TRAPPED AND TACKLED

KNOXVILLE COYOTES FOOTBALL
BOOK 3

GINA AZZI

THREE CITIES PUBLISHING LLC

AUTHOR'S NOTE

Trigger Warning: *Trapped and Tackled* includes depictions of and discussions about domestic violence and an abusive relationship.

"I'm so happy you're back home!" my best friend Marlowe squeals. As her tone reaches peak pitch, my cell phone skitters across the dashboard of Dad's truck and drops to the floor beneath the passenger seat. "Leni?"

"Sorry!" I call out, reaching over to grope for the phone. "I dropped you," I explain as I right myself and slam on the brakes. "Oh my God! I'm so sorry!" I shout, horrified, to the elderly man, cursing me for nearly colliding with him.

After two years of taking the New York City subway, I may have forgotten how to drive.

I ease around him slowly. He leans on his horn, and I wince, feeling my cheeks flame. Another mistake.

"Don't you have Bluetooth?" Marlowe asks. "Your phone should automatically sync when—"

"I've got Dad's truck."

"Ooh," Marlowe breathes out. "You should definitely pay attention to the road."

She's right. The last thing I need is to wreck Dad's truck and cause his and Mom's concern for me to skyrocket higher than it already is. Sighing, I resume my drive to the football training facility where Dad's conducting training camp. "He caught a ride with some players. He called it team bonding."

"Which players?" Marlowe interjects, her tone teasing. She likes to flirt with other guys—especially if it will make her boyfriend Toby jealous. Don't ask me why. Toby's her high school sweetheart who never should have made it past high school.

"Probably Cohen and Avery," I offer, mentioning two of Dad's oldest players. The charismatic wide receiver and celebrated quarterback make up the foundation of the Knoxville Coyotes Football team.

"Meh. I was hoping you would say West Crawford," my boy-crazy friend replies.

I roll my eyes. Last season, Knoxville's rookie West helped win the Super Bowl, and it catapulted him to instant fame. But... "He's having a baby!"

"I know," Marlowe laments. "And his girlfriend has a closet to die for. I swear, they're couple goals."

West Crawford and Nova Martin are more than couple goals. They're...life goals. Fact.

"How long is your car in the shop for?" Marlowe asks.

"Just a few days. Dad's turned it on every now and then, but no one's really driven it for the past two years. Dad wants to check everything before I'm allowed back on the road."

"Good! So you'll be all set for my birthday bash in a few weekends!" Marlowe cheers.

I try to smile, but it falls flat, and shame sweeps through me. I should be excited to celebrate my best friend's birthday. But I'm not in the mood to raise a glass for anything. Or anyone.

Since Craig and I broke up five days ago and I made the tough decision to leave New York and move back home, I have felt like a failure—an epic failure. I'd rather hide than socialize.

I've been home in Knoxville for four days—having returned to my parents' house the night after everything went sideways—and this is the first time I've left the house.

Part of me wonders if my car is fine, and Dad is making

me pick him up just so I see blue sky and breathe some fresh air. It's plausible.

"You are coming, aren't you?" Marlowe asks, and I hear the hurt layered in her tone.

The pit in my stomach expands outward, making me feel nauseous. I clench the steering wheel and roll my shoulders back. "Of course, I'm coming." Thank God my voice doesn't shake. In fact, I sound convincing.

"Good!" Marlowe squeals. "You've missed the last two," she reminds me, unintentionally piling on the guilt.

"I'll be there," I promise.

Marlowe hosts a weekend bash every year at Toby's parents' lakefront home, about an hour and a half from Knoxville. The sunny days are spent out on the lake, the evenings are spent barbecuing, and the nights are spent partying—lots of partying.

"Are you and Freddy grabbing dinner, or do you want to meet Toby and me for pizza?" she asks, switching topics. Except her calling my strict, protective, larger-than-life football coach dad, Friedrich Adler Strauss, her usual nickname Freddy doesn't make me laugh. All I can focus on is that she's inviting me to another outing in which I'll be public-facing.

Forced to smile and talk and act normal.

I swallow, feeling ill at the thought. Gah! I hate how helpless—weak—I am.

It was just a stupid breakup!

It's more than that, my conscience whispers back.

"You wouldn't be third-wheeling it," Marlowe continues before I respond. "Keller's coming too," she mentions her cousin and one of our closest friends.

I clear my throat. "Thanks for the invite, but I'm having dinner with Dad."

"No worries. Now that you're home, we have plenty of time to grab dinners, drinks, and hang out. Ooh, we can even double date!"

I slam on the brakes at her words, causing the guy behind me to swerve around the truck. He honks loudly and flips me the bird.

Shit! I ease the truck to the side of the road and drop my head to the center of the steering wheel, sucking in a gulp of air.

"You know who's hot? Brandon Hensil. Remember him? He was in your creative writing class sophomore year. He's gotten really fit since graduation. Toby's friends with him and can put in a good word. He works at—"

"I'm not ready to date," I manage through clenched teeth.

"Well, maybe not this week since the idea of Craig is still fresh, but…"

I tune Marlowe out as the pit of my stomach slicks with nausea, and my throat closes. The last person I'd let set me up on a date is Toby, but it's the mention of Craig that cuts. Just hearing his name makes the backs of my eyelids burn with unshed tears.

We met the month after my college graduation, and I fell for him instantly. It was one of those sappy, love-at-first-sight connections I always dreamed would happen to me. And then, it did.

The same week I started my full-time employment at Henley Events, I moved in with Craig.

Those first six months were pure bliss. I guess we were playing house, but nothing had ever felt more real to me.

Safe, steady, and reliable.

He was a finance guy who worked on Wall Street. Nothing like the rowdy, good-time football players my dad warned me to stay away from.

Craig may not bench-press two hundred twenty-five pounds or throw the perfect spiral, but he's a business-minded visionary who prefers stability—at least, I thought he did.

It's funny how athletes get the party-guy reputations, but

the Wall Street bros who swirl scotch and casually snort cocaine are viewed as "clean-cut." Either way, things began to spiral until, five nights ago, it all went horribly wrong. I called Mom early the next morning and came straight home.

And since I've been back, the harsh reality of life with Craig has trailed after me. The memories and his random text messages that continue to set me on edge—reminding me that even though I've left New York, I haven't escaped him. Not entirely.

Mom and Dad know there's more to the story than my being homesick, and I'm still unsure how much to confide in them. I'm unsure how much to confide in anyone, which is why I haven't said anything to Marlowe either. Instead, I put space between us.

As Marlowe continues to chat, I ease back onto the road.

I'll have to decide quickly because dinner with Dad promises to be an inquisition. In fact, I'm surprised he's given me four days to adjust to being home. I'm sure that was at Mom's urging to allow me some time, but Coach Strauss isn't a patient man when it comes to his daughters' well-being.

Physically, I'm talking to my best friend.

Mentally, I'm preparing for dinner with Dad.

Emotionally, I'm teetering on the edge.

Should I have left Craig sooner? Am I a failure for leaving New York and a job at a top agency in the city? Was I too naïve and trusting, and should I have known better from the start?

"Ooh, I gotta go! That's Toby!" Marlowe interrupts herself.

I blink back unbidden tears. "No worries, Mar," I mutter. "I'm nearly here anyway," I add as I turn into the parking lot of the training facility. "Talk to you later?"

"Yes, I'll call you. Say hey to Freddy, and don't forget to tell him about my birthday weekend." She disconnects.

I navigate Dad's truck into his designated parking spot.

Turning off the ignition, I breathe out a shaky exhale and try to shore up some resolve. Some gumption.

I used to live for dinners with Dad. And the truth is, I miss him and hate the distance that's grown between us since I moved away. It wasn't the city that caused the space... It was Craig. No, it was the version I became from being with Craig.

Grabbing my purse, I slide from the truck and call Dad.

"Hey!" his deep voice answers.

"Hi, Dad. I'm here," I say.

"Good, good. I'm just wrapping up a few things."

Of course, he is. My dad is fully committed to this team, and he's always "wrapping things up." It could mean another ten minutes or another two hours. "No problem."

"I'll send a player out to bring you up."

"Okay," I agree, my nerves rattling at the thought of interacting one-on-one with a big, burly football player.

I've been gone for two years, and save for a handful of the older guys, the Coyotes boasts a newer roster. If he sends a player I don't know, what will we talk about? What will I say?

And when did I forget how to make small talk?

"Head to the main entrance, and I'll see you soon."

"See you." I click off and turn in the direction of the main entrance.

It's hot outside, but I relish the sunshine on my skin. For years, New York City was my dream. Fast-paced bustle, high-profile events, and big rewards. Bright lights and shimmering possibilities.

But somewhere over the last two years, I realized I didn't quite fit, and I didn't care. I missed blue skies and sunshine, flowy dresses and flower crowns, tailgates and Friday night lights.

I missed my home and my family and the familiar.

My Wall Street boyfriend, the job at the fancy agency, and

the apartment with a view of Central Park started to pale in comparison to my hometown.

I'm still struggling to admit that out loud. Somewhere in my mind, I hear Craig scoff at my being "basic."

I reach the main entrance, and the glass door swings open as a guy steps outside.

I look up and freeze as I come face-to-face with Talon Miller. He's the Coyotes star kicker. A fun-loving, smirking, wild player who seems to be the life of every party. He made some headlines after the Coyotes won the Super Bowl, and while Dad grumbled about it, he did so with a grin, letting me know he thinks Miller's all right.

I've seen him several times but don't know him—not how I know Cohen Campbell and Avery Callaway. Miller's newer to the team, playing for two or three seasons, and I've been gone for most of them.

Still, I recognize every Coyotes player on sight and can probably rattle off their stats since my father's job tends to appear in most of our conversations.

Even more so as I ran out of things to tell him on our weekly phone calls. But if I confided in Dad, he'd be on the next flight to New York.

While most, if not all, of the Coyotes players are good-looking, something about Talon Miller makes me catch my breath.

He's tall and lean, with broad shoulders and a tapered waist. He has reddish-brown hair, cropped close to the sides of his head and left longer on top. Several days of stubble coat his jawline. His full lips quirk into a grin. And his eyes—gray with flecks of green—dance playfully.

He's nothing like Craig, and as my heart kicks behind my breastbone, a stirring of attraction that I haven't felt in weeks —months?—flares to life.

I breathe out a sigh of relief that I can still feel something for a man. That I'm not broken.

"I'm finally meeting Leni Strauss," he says by way of greeting, holding out a hand.

I smile gratefully and place my hand in his, ignoring how large his palm is. His fingers are warm as they wrap around mine. "It's good to officially meet you, Talon."

His mouth turns up at the corners, and he releases my hand. I slip it behind my back, aware it still tingles from his touch.

"Your dad's thrilled you're back," he says kindly. All it does is make me feel worse for staying away as long as I did. Talon holds the door open and glances at me. "Are you planning to stay in Knoxville for good?"

Already, the questions start. I know he means them harmlessly—he's just making small talk. But my heart thumps in my eardrums, and my vision narrows.

Yes. I can't go back to the city.

The words spin in my mind and sit on the tip of my tongue, but I can't say them aloud.

I shouldn't let a breakup keep me from a city I love. But it's more than that, and no one truly understands.

I slip inside, and he follows.

For good. It sounds so permanent, and yet… I guess it's the truth. I haven't had much time to process this new life change.

"That's the plan," I reply, my tone too bright. Fake.

He bumps his arm lightly against my shoulder. I stiffen from the contact, a rush of nerves skittering through me. "Happy about it? Or was it hard to leave the big city lights behind?"

I glance up at him, unable to tell if he's teasing me. His tone is too familiar—after all, we've never met. And yet, his questions already prick at things I'm hiding beneath the surface.

He gazes down, his eyes sincere.

"A mix of both," I answer honestly. "It's…bittersweet."

He sighs and nods as if understanding the meaning behind my words. "Hopefully, more sweet than bitter."

"We'll see," I breathe out.

He regards me again, his eyes studying my face, perusing my features as if he's searching something out. What? A reaction, an emotion?

Does he know? Can he tell?

My eyebrows tug together, confused by our exchange. It's nothing, and yet…it feels like something. I can't figure it out. Can't figure him out.

"Well, your timing is perfect," he says as he presses the call button for the elevator. Lowering his voice, he quips, "Your Dad went a bit easier on us today." He grins, and his eyes spark. He's playful and easygoing, so different from the intensity Craig always exuded.

"Glad I could help," I reply, surprised by how comfortable I feel around him.

The doors open immediately, and we step inside.

Talon tilts his head and presses the button for floor three. "He missed you."

I look up, taken aback again. It's an expected remark, yet Talon says it as if he truly knows Dad. As if he understands Dad's joy at having his daughter back home.

"Yeah," I agree. "I missed him, too."

Talon nods, his grin growing. "Now, if your sister decides to return from Germany, Coach may dance in the end zone."

I chuckle, the sound jarring as it falls from my lips. I press my fingertips to my mouth. When was the last time I laughed? About anything?

Talon grins back and widens his stance, casually crossing his arms over his chest.

His body heat skates over my skin, and his scent—soap, a hint of cologne, and mint—washes over me. Enclosed with Talon in the elevator, I realize how close we're standing. I wrap my arms around my middle.

"I've always wanted to go overseas," he offers, pulling me out of my thoughts.

"You've never been?"

He snorts, the sound more amused than annoyed. "Nah."

The doors open again, and I step out slightly ahead of him.

"Never even dreamed about places like Europe before the Coyotes. And since joining the team…" He shrugs.

I want to ask him what that means. Why hasn't he taken a trip?

"There's my girl!" Dad's voice rumbles over me.

Talon shuffles back a step as I turn and smile at Dad. He walks toward me, his arms outstretched, as if it's been weeks since he's seen me instead of at breakfast this morning.

I meet him halfway, hugging him hello. "Your truck is fine," I assure him.

Dad tips his head back and laughs, probably relieved I'm still capable of joking. "Thank God. I was getting worried."

"You were not." I smack his arm lightly.

I step out of Dad's embrace and note Talon studying us, a line pinched between his brows.

"You met Miller," Dad grunts.

"Yep," I say.

Talon dips his chin, his eyes still on me. "See you around, Leni," he says easily. Casually.

And yet, something about his tone tugs deep in my stomach.

Something about him unnerves me, and I have no idea what it is.

"See you," I reply.

Talon glances at Dad. "Until tomorrow, Coach."

"Take it easy, Miller," Dad replies, looking down at me. "You hungry?"

"Starving," I admit. I've barely eaten today. Or for the past few days. Maybe longer.

But from the corner of my eye, I watch as Talon retreats. Even steps, casual gait, and…swagger.

For years, I've found my dad's players handsome. But Talon Miller is downright hot. Sinful. Sexy.

And the realization is more than surprising.

It's alarming.

Confusing.

"Good. A new steakhouse just opened not too far from here," Dad continues. "Let me grab my bag from the office."

"Okay."

Talon pushes into the stairwell, but he glances back right before he steps through. Our eyes connect.

Stormy gray thunderclouds hold me hostage.

I suck in a breath, and that smirk tugs across his full mouth.

Then, he enters the stairwell, the door swings closed, and I remember to breathe.

Dangerous.

2
TALON

She's charming in a sweet, innocent way. Like the girl-next-door, she has no idea how beautiful she is.

Damn. I shake my head.

The last woman I need to be thinking about is Coach's fucking daughter.

I met his other daughter, Lincoln Strauss, after the Super Bowl last year and while I caught a glimpse of Leni when Lincoln pointed her out, it was from a distance. All I saw was her blonde hair and a bit of the blue dress she was wearing.

Lincoln's gorgeous and she knows it. She brims with confidence. Older, wiser, and smart as hell.

Leni's softer. Sweeter. Lovelier.

Lovelier? I shake my head.

What the fuck is wrong with me?

Coach adores his girls. It was one of the first things I learned about him, from the first time I entered his office and saw a framed photo of his family. His stunning wife, Vicki, and their two bright-eyed, blonde girls—Lincoln and Leni.

And then, the pieces of them he shared with me during my first year as one of his players.

I pause in the stairwell, gripping the banister to pull in a breath.

I haven't thought about that year, those stretch of weeks

that were so short, yet etched in my brain for eternity, in a long time.

I only had my mother in my life for a handful of years. The first three—which I barely remember save for the sound of smacks and the silhouette of her cowering on the bathroom floor—before Child Protective Services intervened and I ended up in the foster care system. And a five-and-a-half week stretch when I was a rookie for the Coyotes, my mother was dying, and Coach Strauss intervened to help me say goodbye.

Then, he helped me organize her funeral and stood by my side, squeezing my shoulder, as her casket was lowered into the ground.

To my knowledge, he never told anyone. And neither did I.

But the long hours he kept me company at my mother's bedside, he shared snippets of his personal life. His family life.

I learned about his family's immigration from Germany to America. Then, the found family he sought in football—not unlike my own experience. The woman who captured his heart—a sweet debutante from a prominent Tennessee family, Victoria, affectionately known as Vicki. And the two little girls who made him a dad—Lincoln and Leni. While he shared stories of both his daughters, the ones about Leni made me laugh.

The way she colored her doll's faces with markers and pretended it was makeup when she was six. How she continued to host a wedding reception that all her dolls, stuffed animals, and family were forced to attend.

Another story, about when Lincoln dared Leni to slide down the banister at a country club and she ended up with eleven stitches along her hairline.

There was the time she cut bangs at twelve because some

punk told her she had a fivehead and she cried herself to sleep, holding the chunk of her cut hair.

The first time she got drunk at a lake house and called Vicki, begging to pick her up. But first made her swear not to rat out any of her friends to their parents.

From the stories Coach shared, I deduced that Leni is trouble adjacent. She never intends to find herself in a sticky situation but because she's Lincoln's sister and some girl Marlowe's best friend, she's usually along for the ride. She's loyal and loving.

I enjoyed listening to Coach's stories about Leni. They were wholesome and sincere. They were so unlike my own childhood, they almost sounded made up.

In fact, if it wasn't Coach telling them, I would have called bullshit.

But during those confusing weeks when I had to find closure with a mother who never wanted me, grapple for my footing with a team that was my ticket to a future, and perform on the field—the stories about sweet, quirky, sunny Leni made me smile.

They made me believe in a type of goodness I've only caught glimpses of over the years.

She made me realize that there are women out there who aren't after a player because of the job title or the money or the social status. There are women who just believe in love.

Imagine that?

Shaking my head at my wayward thoughts, I bound down the steps, and swing by the cafeteria for a shot of espresso. I have one more meeting with Coach Stevens before I head home.

Training camp has kicked off and I can't afford distractions. Or missteps. This team—Coach Strauss specifically—has taken me under their wing and molded me into the player I am today.

A kicker who helped win the Super Bowl last season.

It's a legacy I'd like to uphold. It's the only thing I truly have to my name. Without football—who am I? What am I?

I'm a kid from Indiana who grew up solo, with a chip on my shoulder, and found an outlet in a game I love. That game bought me an education and a career and a team. A family.

I can't sacrifice that for anything.

I take a sip of my espresso and check my Apple Watch. Ten minutes left.

"Yo," Gage Gutierrez calls out.

I glance up and flip my chin in his direction. Sauntering over to the cafeteria table a few of my teammates are seated around, I drop down.

"What are you still doing here?" Jag Baglione asks.

I lean back in my chair. "Meeting with Stevens in a few."

"Hey," our wide receiver, Cohen Campbell, glances at our QB, Avery Callaway. "You think Leni showed up yet?"

"She did," I confirm, before I realize he wasn't asking me.

The guys at the table swing their gazes my way. I take another sip of espresso. Clear my throat. "Coach asked me to meet her at the main entrance and bring her up to his office until he finished a call."

Avery shakes his head at me. "Don't get any ideas, Miller. Leni Strauss is off-fucking-limits."

Cohen scoffs. "He wasn't getting ideas. Talon's not that stupid."

West Crawford tilts his head, pondering this assumption. "You sure?"

I flip him the middle finger. "She seems like a nice girl."

"Ah, Len's the best," Cohen says sincerely. "Lincoln too. When they were in high school, Coach made them come to every home game."

"Every pep rally, every charity event," Callaway tacks on.

"He pointed out how smelly and gross we are." Cohen laughs, gesturing around the table. "The stench of our pads—"

"The piles of dirty towels," Avery adds.

"Anything he could to steer those girls away from football players," Cohen continues.

"Hell, athletes in general." Avery nods. "Not that I blame coach. If I had a daughter, I wouldn't want her anywhere near us."

"Speak for yourself," Leo Quincy quips, sliding into a chair next to West. "Crawford's got a kid and—"

"Nope," West interjects. "Callaway's right. I don't want my baby girl anywhere near a football team when she grows up."

The guys laugh and I force a grin, but something pulls tight in my chest.

I know they're joking around—with a modicum of truth. But it's the truth that cuts. Because no dad would want me around their daughter. Especially not a father like Coach Strauss. And definitely not a daughter like sunny Leni.

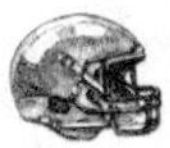

"More time in the swimming pool," I repeat Coach Stevens' words.

"It's good for resistance training. Not to mention, recovery," Coach Stevens explains. "As we segue from training camp into preseason, I want you to make it part of your conditioning routine. You don't always have to come out this way. It's fine if you want to hit a pool in the city."

"Got it," I confirm, feeling a headache forming.

Today was a long day and while I don't expect any less from training camp, incorporating additional pool time and strength-training exercises is another thing to stack into my routine.

"All good, Miller?" Stevens presses, looking at me curiously.

I rap my knuckles against the edge of his desk and stand. "Great." I flash a smirk and shoulder my bag. "See you tomorrow."

"Bright and early."

"Yep," I say, leaving his office.

By the time I drive home and collapse onto my couch, I'm beat. And I don't know why. The physical intensity and demanding rigor of training camp is nothing new. I've stayed in shape and continued my conditioning since the season ended, not counting a month or two that I spent reveling in our Super Bowl win.

There were parties. Wild events. And willing women.

It was chaotic fun. A high I'd never experienced before.

But now it's over and…there's a mental toll that's hitting me. I wasn't prepared for it but I'm tired. Drained.

Lonely.

I pick up my phone to scroll through some social media accounts. Weddings, puppies, newborn babies, and cute toddlers with pigtails. Most of my teammates from the University of Oregon have settled down. They've found jobs coaching or in broadcasting. A few became finance or tech guys. They've purchased homes with expansive properties and swimming pools. Some of them have gotten married and started a family. Others have adopted rescue dogs and spend their weekends hiking or mountain biking. A handful have scattered across the US, or gone abroad, for employment.

Hell, even the guys on my team are moving forward.

West has Nova and their sweet baby girl.

Cohen's tied up with Raia.

Avery's got a new flavor of the week nearly every week.

Quincy is dating some single mom he's had the hots for since high school.

Who knows what the hell Jag does but he's not around often.

And Gutierrez is tight with his family so even if he's not

actively dating, he's also not sitting on his couch alone ninety-nine percent of the time.

Sighing, I tip my head back and drop my phone.

I hate how melancholy I feel. I hate that the highlight of my day was meeting Coach's daughter and finally putting a face to the quirky girl who tried to paint Coach's nails in team colors before his first coaching gig.

I detest the way my body reacted to seeing her. The lightness that spread through my limbs. The hope that expanded in my chest.

Damn. I squeeze my eyes shut. There's something wrong with me.

Forcing myself to stand from the couch, I make my way to the kitchen and microwave some chicken breast and broccoli I meal-prepped on Sunday.

Then I sit down and eat dinner alone—the way I do most nights. I prepare my bag for camp tomorrow. I look up the free swim schedule at the city pool.

And I go to sleep. Even though I'm physically exhausted and mentally screwed up, I can't fight the thoughts of a sweet blonde I have no business thinking about.

3

Leni

"Don't get any ideas about my players now that you're back," Dad warns, pointing a French fry at me. "And single."

He's baiting me.

I don't fall for it. "Mom says you need to lay off the fried food."

His eyes narrow. "Don't change the subject."

"I'm not." I flick my fingers at him before popping one of his fries into my mouth. "You needing to prioritize your health is a fact."

He glowers. I grin.

"And," I reassure him, "I'm not going to suddenly fall for one of your players when you've been warning Linc and me away from the team since we were like fifteen."

"My rules stand," Dad carries on. "Just because you're an adult now—"

"I've been an adult since I turned eighteen," I remind him, pausing to take a swig of my Diet Coke.

"You're still living under my roof. And my rules stand."

I smirk, loving how much he cares. While Craig's interference in my personal life came from a place of control, Dad's comes from a place of love. "I know, Dad. I got it."

"Good," he grunts. And then, "How torn up are you over Craig?"

I sigh, letting my shoulders slump. "Mom told you to ask, huh?"

Dad nods in confirmation. "But even I know when you're hurting, Leni Lou." He uses the nickname my parents used to call me as a kid to soften the blow this topic delivers. "I know you're putting on a brave face."

I nod, blinking to keep my tears at bay. The truth is, I'm not that good at putting on a brave face. Or pretending everything is cool when it's not. Or acting like my heart isn't shattered and my dreams aren't splintering. But are they? "I thought I was going to marry him." My voice cracks and Dad winces.

"I know," he murmurs, reaching across the table to place his large, rough hand on mine. "He seemed like a good one. What happened anyway?"

I sigh, biting my bottom lip. My parents don't know how many hours Craig worked. How some nights, he wouldn't come home until three a.m., reeking of booze, his eyes too bright.

They don't know how controlling he became, commenting on my choices of clothing and inspecting my makeup to ensure my lipstick was demure, not bold.

The more he worked, the more he drank. And the more he drank, the more a mean streak emerged.

But I can't tell my father that. He'd head up to the city and beat the piss out of Craig.

Besides, my hurt over things going sideways also stems from my guilt in staying with Craig for as long as I did. I naively hoped things would change. I thought that if I could be enough for him, he would fight for me. For us.

I wanted to be the reason he got help and got better. By conjuring that mental fantasy where my love for him would be enough to inspire a change, I allowed myself to stay in a dangerous situation.

But the gash on my arm and the bruises on my neck were

the last straw. The one that broke the camel's back, buckled my knees, and nudged me to call Mom.

I don't want to share that with Dad. I don't want to admit that I stayed with Craig through the shouting matches and the night he threw a bottle of scotch against the wall. The time he slapped me across the face. I don't want to tell him how I started cutting off my friendships, ignoring Marlowe, and sending Lincoln's calls to voicemail. Or growing unbearably homesick and not knowing how to vocalize it.

I've failed at everything I pursued in the city and now I'm back home, with my tail between my legs. I don't know where to go from here.

In response to his question, I shrug. "We…grew apart," I reply lamely, layering my lie with a tiny morsel of truth.

"Hm," Dad murmurs, watching me closely. "That happens sometimes."

"Yeah." I take a bite of my steak. I know it's delicious, but I hardly taste it. Not with my stomach in knots and my knee bouncing beneath the table.

Dad wipes his mouth with a folded napkin and regards me carefully. "You know you can talk to me about anything, right, Len?"

I nod, tears burning the backs of my eyelids. "I know."

"I won't judge you." Dad pauses. "Too hard anyway."

I snort. "I'm sure."

He grins, then shakes his head. "We all make mistakes. The important thing is to learn from them. But Craig, he seemed solid. A smart, ambitious, reliable man."

"Yeah," I whisper, my throat tightening. "He seemed like a lot of things."

Dad stares at me curiously before polishing off his T-bone.

Before he can press me further, I blurt out, "Marlowe's celebrating her birthday at Toby's parents' place on the lake in a few weekends."

Dad quirks an eyebrow.

"Your house, your rules..." I prompt, letting him know that I'm looking for him to give me the go-ahead even though I hardly need it.

He sighs and wipes a palm over the lower half of his face. "She's still with Toby, huh?"

"On and off," I confirm.

Dad nods. "Let me think about it."

"Dad—"

"I know you don't need my permission, Len, but I appreciate you checking in anyway. Just, let me think things over, okay?"

"Okay," I agree as the server stops at the end of the table.

Dad asks for the check and settles the bill.

We ride home together, listening to some throwback music and talking easily. When we enter our house, Dad kisses the top of my head and disappears into his office.

I find a note from Mom that she joined a friend for dinner since Dad and I went out for a bite.

Sighing, I plop down on a barstool at the kitchen island and pull out my phone. Life here is quieter...simpler...than it was in the city. There, I felt a need to keep up appearances.

My evenings were spent preparing for Craig to return from work. I used to cook his favorite meals and try my hand at crafting cocktails. I would set the table with a different aesthetic or play with my makeup and hair.

I kept thinking that if I could get it right, be what he wanted me to be, things would get better.

I practically burned out from trying so hard and things only worsened.

This is a fresh start. A new beginning.

I drop into my bed and stare up at the ceiling. I always wanted to be an event planner, a wedding planner, specifically. To help create a vision for two people on the brink of creating one life. To celebrate their love.

My friends used to tease me for being a hopeless romantic.

These days, I just feel hopeless.

Sighing, I close my eyes and drift off to sleep.

"Wake up, Leni Lou!" Mom tugs the curtains in my room wide open, letting the sunlight stream in.

"Mom!" I groan, clapping a hand over my face.

I sit up groggily and glare at her.

She beams and claps her hands together. "I have the perfect project for you to get out of this funk."

Funk. I wince, absently rubbing along my collarbone where Craig's nails bit into my skin. Where the tightness of his hold on my throat left bruises. "What is it?"

"The Clarke Country Club Debutante Ball!" Mom squeals.

Oh, gosh. My mouth drops open. "Mom! That's an actual event," I hiss. It's one my mother participated in years ago, when she was seventeen years old. Since then, she's faithfully served on the organizing committee. But when she asked Lincoln and me to participate in the debutante ball, we both respectfully declined.

It was too…serious for me then. And now, with my life in shambles, I'm even less qualified to participate in an event of that magnitude. Even as a member of the planning committee. Even as a volunteer.

"I know." Her smile softens. "I had dinner with Marylee Picolin last night and she told me that Claire Tipton—"

"The Claire Tipton," I repeat, emphasizing *Tipton*. The Tipton family has hosted and organized the event for as long as I can remember.

Mom sits on the edge of my bed and reaches for my hand. "Claire is expecting her first baby and was just put on bedrest. She's in no shape to oversee the event and needs her mom and sisters to help her over the next few months. As a result, the organizing committee is taking on new members. And here you are—with a wealth of New York City experience under your belt."

"It was one year," I remind her.

"Plus a year of interning." She holds up two fingers. "It could be a great opportunity for you, Len. You'd network with so many of the town's families. And with weddings becoming more and more popular in Tennessee…"

I sigh, knowing she's right. I tuck my hair behind my ears. "Do you really think I have anything to offer?"

Mom's eyebrows tug together and her smile slips. "Of course I do. The question is why you don't? Leni, you are talented, creative, and compassionate. There's nothing you can't do." Spoken like a true mother.

I arch an eyebrow.

"The committee's been planning for months. Now, it's more about final details and execution." Mom taps my hip. "Come on, get up. We're meeting the ladies at the country club in an hour."

"You agreed that I'd join?!" I gasp.

Mom tilts her head, studying me. Then, she stands. "A year ago, you would have jumped at the chance."

Disappointment swirls in my stomach as my fingers clench the hem of my sheet. Mom's right. A year ago, I would already be in the shower, mentally creating a vision board for the event. Table decor and flower arrangements. Table layouts and a menu.

But…the debutante ball is a big deal. What if I suggest an idea and it flops? What if I disappoint the Tiptons? What if—

"What's going on, Len?" Mom's tone is softer. Her eyes… worried.

Guilt expands in my chest, traveling up my throat until I feel sick. The last thing I want is to worry my mom. To disappoint her.

"Nothing." I shake my head, swinging my legs to the side of my bed. "I'll shower and get ready to go."

I stand and my knees nearly buckle beneath me. I dash into the bathroom, slamming into the vanity as soon as the door is closed behind me.

Black dots flicker in the periphery of my vision and the taste of adrenaline floods my mouth.

Bracing my arms on the ledge of the vanity, I suck in deep breaths. The edge of a panic attack shimmers around me as my heart rate skyrockets.

I hold the ledge of the vanity tightly, forcing myself to get a grip on reality.

Everything is fine. I'm fine.

I'm not going to fail at this. I'm not a failure.

"Leni." Mom knocks on the bathroom door.

Shit. I meet my wild, unfocused eyes in the mirror and wince. Working a swallow, I turn and flip on the showerhead. The running water soothes me as much as it drowns out the sound of my ragged breathing.

What if I ruin the ball? What if I have no ideas? What was Mom thinking?

"Yes?" I heave over the sink.

"I left a dress on your bed. I think it will look beautiful on you."

Tears prick the corners of my eyes as I pull in air. "Thanks, Mama."

I haven't called her mama in years, and I know the moment she hears it because her gasp is audible.

Silence hangs between us and I can feel her presence, standing, waiting, just outside the bathroom door.

I take in another breath, get my thoughts under control, and slowly pull myself together. Then, I step into the shower and scrub until my body and mind are clean once more.

"Leni Strauss! You look amazing!" Marylee Picolin announces.

I blush under her praise and kiss her cheeks in greeting. "How are you, Marylee?"

"Wonderful, darling." She lowers her voice. "But you must tell me your secret. You must be a size two now!"

I drop my chin, forcing a smile.

Anxiety, guilt, and failure will do that to a woman. Not a weight loss cocktail I recommend.

Of course, I don't say that. I just titter a laugh and let her lead me to the waiting table of women.

"Welcome home, Leni! We missed you." Anna Louise Shreider waves.

The warmth with which the women receive me eases some of my panic. Mom and I sit down at the table with the perfectly coiffed society ladies. We exchange greetings, fix our tea, and get down to business.

As Marylee explains the event, the vision, and their current plans, I begin to relax. The debutante ball—while a staple in our town—isn't as elaborate as some of the weddings I helped bring to life for Manhattan's high society.

When we start to discuss the design aesthetic, I jump in with suggestions that the women gobble up. Beside me, the tension Mom was holding in her shoulders and back ease. Beneath the table, I reach for her hand, and she finds mine, squeezing my fingers reassuringly.

I press my thanks into her palm and know that she operated with my best interests at heart.

I can do this; I can help plan Knoxville's debutante ball.

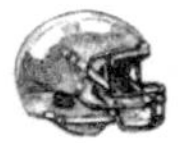

Craig: I miss you, Leni.

My heart rate ticks up at Craig's text message, and I grip my phone tighter. I scan the thread of our exchanges, noting that my last reply was before that night. Before I left. And still, he continues to message me.

He's relentless.

Shaking my head, I try to brush off the panic that sparks with any mention of Craig. There are hundreds of miles between us and I'm safe, here in my hometown, in my parents' house.

After a busy day and a leisurely lunch with Mom, I feel more like myself than I have in a year. I'm more relaxed, less on edge, and filled with energy.

There's no way I'm letting Craig—and the memory of what was—ruin it.

In my room, I tug on my swimsuit and toss a towel, goggles, and an old swim cap into a backpack.

"Dad!" I call out, knowing he's busy at work in his office. "I'm heading to the pool to get some laps in. I'm taking your truck."

"Drive carefully!" he yells back.

I swipe his keys from the hook by the door, fingering the little AirTag attached to his keyring for all the times he misplaces them, and make my way to his truck.

I blast music on the ride to the community pool, singing along at the top of my lungs and laughing to myself. When was the last time I felt this carefree?

This...happy and excited for the future?

After stowing my items in the locker room, I make my way out to the pool, snag an empty lane, and dive into the cool water. It sluices over me as I come up for air, inhaling deeply. Then, I swim laps, allowing myself to get lost in the comfortable, monotonous strokes. My mind clears, my breathing evens out, and I settle into a steady pace, relishing the feel of my body cutting through the water.

At least, until I take a break at the wall, look to the left, and come face-to-face with Talon Miller.

"Sunny Leni." He grins.

Sunny Leni? My heart rate increases as I grip the side of the pool.

Does he have a nickname for me?

"What are you doing here?" I ask.

"Same as you," he says, gesturing toward the pool. His eyes—more green than gray in the pool water—spark with amusement. "Swimming laps."

I force myself not to look down and check him out. Which is harder than it should be.

"Yeah. I mean, I've never seen you here before."

He quirks an eyebrow. "Haven't you only been home a few days?"

I dip my head, feeling my cheeks redden.

I've never seen you here before. What a dumb thing to say!

"Stevens added more pool time to my schedule," Talon explains.

"Oh," I say, feeling embarrassed.

"You look good out there, Len."

Surprise fans out in my chest, mixing with disbelief. "I do?"

I expect him to flip a joke my way. Instead, he regards me seriously. "You're a strong swimmer. Couldn't take my eyes off you."

My throat dries at the sincerity in his gaze, and I work a swallow. "Oh. Um, I—"

One side of Talon's mouth ticks up as he grips the wall beside me and hoists himself out of the pool. "Don't let me keep you."

"No, you're not," I sputter, unsure what to say.

Besides, any words I was capable of speaking have fled

my mind. Because now I'm looking up at Talon. And, my God, is he a sight.

Water droplets slide down the length of his strong, hard body. His quads are thick and his wet bathing suit sticks to them, outlining his muscles. His abs ripple, the droplets of water tossing the reflection of the fluorescent lights. Broad shoulders flex as he reaches for a towel. He drags it over his hair, closing his eyes, and I fight the moan that climbs up my throat.

Is he doing this on purpose? To tease me? He must know how hot he is... He must know the effect he has on people in his immediate vicinity. He's striking without trying to be.

And what is wrong with me, ogling this man like he's up for grabs. Like I'd ever be in his orbit to grab him.

He's strong enough to crush me and while that should warn me to stay away, I find myself mesmerized by him.

I press my thighs together, relieved he can't see as I hug the pool wall. I clear my throat. "I'm done too." I push up, hoisting myself out of the pool.

My one-piece bathing suit is simple. Black with thin straps.

It's one Craig made me purchase when he learned about my early morning swims at the gym.

But Talon Miller stares at me, drinks me in, like I'm rocking a string bikini.

Awareness spikes through my body and desire beckons. My nipples pebble from the cold—or maybe his attention?—and his gaze drops to my chest.

I wrap my arm around my middle, unsure what to do next. *Do I reach for my towel? Yank off my swim cap?*

Talon puts a stop to my spiraling thoughts by scooping up my towel and holding it open before wrapping it around my shoulders.

"Thanks," I say as I pull off my swim cap, gripping it in

the same hand as my goggles. My other hand tugs out my hair tie and my damp hair tumbles around my shoulders.

Talon makes a sound in the back of his throat, and I look up.

His eyes are darker than they were a second ago. The green has been eaten by slate and steel.

I blink and he looks away, gripping the back of his neck.

"You need a ride home, Leni?" he offers, his voice huskier.

I shake my head. "I have Dad's truck."

Talon clears his throat and tosses his towel over one shoulder. "Okay."

He moves to turn around and suddenly, I don't want him to go.

Today was a good day, the best day I've had in a while, and I don't want to go home and be alone. I don't want to think about the past or wonder when Craig will text again.

"I'm going to get some ice cream," I sputter, feeling like a dolt the second the words are out of my mouth.

Talon pauses and glances at me over his shoulder. His gaze is intense, his eyebrows pulled together with a little line forming in the center. "I like ice cream."

I work a swallow, shuffling from one foot to the next. "Do you want to…get an ice cream cone with me?"

My God. I cringe at how desperate I sound. Pathetic. Childish.

Talon turns to face me fully and my eyes drop to his chest. To his washboard abs. To his golden skin.

He steps toward me, and I watch as his feet near mine.

His finger curls beneath my chin and he gently lifts my face to his.

I forget to breathe as Talon studies me. Searches my eyes. Digs beneath my expression. Looks at me and sees more than I want to show. He drops his hand, and I wince, preparing myself for his rejection.

What the hell was I thinking? It was stupid.

"I—" I begin to backtrack.

Talon's expression softens and his eyes spark with flecks of moss green. "Yeah, I'd love to take you for an ice cream cone, Sunny Leni."

He would? The pressure in my stomach eases as I let out an exhale brimming with relief. A smile slowly spreads across my mouth as my new nickname registers.

Sunny Leni. He said it again and even though I don't understand why he chose that nickname, I like that he gifted it to me.

I like that he equates me with sunshine. I haven't felt like that woman in years but being around Talon, even these brief encounters, reminds me that a long time ago, I was positive and hopeful. Sunny.

Talon shakes his head before reaching for my hand. He tugs me toward the locker rooms.

"Come on," he says, pushing the women's door open for me and holding it while I slip through. "I'll wait for you out front."

"Okay," I agree. The swinging door closes behind me.

Then, I rush to my locker, relieved I brought shampoo and conditioner. I shower quickly, pull on the summer dress and sandals I packed, and finger comb my hair before blasting it with a blow-dryer so it's not soaking wet. I braid it quickly, swipe lip gloss across my lips, and study my reflection.

It's hardly a date since I'm not ready to date. Besides, I could never be with one of Dad's football players. But it's the cherry on top of today and right now, I'm holding on to this feeling of lightness with both hands.

4
TALON

"WHAT ARE YOUR PLANS NOW THAT YOU'RE BACK?" I BLURT OUT the question as she places a spoonful of pralines-and-cream ice cream between her plump lips.

Her eyes widen and she opens her mouth, a bit of ice cream falling to the corner of her bottom lip. "I—sorry, what?"

She's cute when she's flustered. Using my thumb to swipe away the bit of ice cream, I repeat my question.

Leni clears her throat, glancing around uncertainly. It's not the first time I've noticed her looking lost—anxious—and usually in response to general questions. "I met with the women who organize the debutante ball today."

I tilt my head, waiting for more of an explanation. "The debutante ball?"

She flushes. "Yes. It's an annual coming-out party for women of age."

"Huh?" I mutter. "Like, some nineteenth-century shit?"

She snorts, rubbing the tip of her nose. "Kind of. But not." She shakes her head. "I'm explaining this terribly. Historically speaking, yes, a debutante ball was when a woman of marrying age entered society and let suitors know she was ready for marriage. But today, it's more focused on women's empowerment, philanthropy for notable charities, and continuing traditions that foster community. Here in Knoxville, well, it's Southern," she tacks on, making me smirk.

"I figured."

Leni chuckles and her shoulders drop an inch. It's the most relaxed I've seen her, with pink dotting her cheeks and her cerulean eyes glowing. She looks beautiful. Breathtaking.

Off-fucking-limits.

I clear my throat. "So, you met with the women who organize it?"

"Yes," she continues, nodding. "My mom arranged for me to join the organizing committee. Back in New York, I worked in event planning. Now that I'm home, trying to figure things out, Mom thought this would be a step in the right direction."

"What do you think?" I wonder.

She bites the corner of her lip. "I was worried I'd fail at it," she murmurs quietly. Honestly. It cuts me up how damn willing she is to make herself vulnerable and admit the truth. It's something I'd never fucking do. "But I think it is a step forward. I need to do something, right?" She looks to me and for a second, it's as if she's seeking my confirmation.

"If this is what you want to do, then I'm sure you'll make it a huge success," I say easily. Truthfully. I don't doubt that Leni takes her career seriously. Coach always said she was studious and disciplined. Seeing her swim laps, listening to her admit her fears, confirms that.

"I hope so," she sighs, taking another bite of ice cream. "What about you? How are you feeling about preseason?"

The subject change to football is common ground. Not to mention, a safe topic.

As I tell her about training camp and we talk about the team, I note three things.

One, she's easy to talk to. A hell of a lot easier than most women I've conversed with.

Two, she's skittish. Unsure of herself, which is at odds

with everything Coach has shared about her. But it's clear she's trying to find her way.

And three, I need to stay the hell away from Sunny Leni. Because the more she talks, the more I find myself falling into her deep blue eyes. Thinking about how silky her hair would feel against my fingertips. And wondering what her lips taste like.

It goes against everything I believe in—loyalty. The only thing I own is my name and I've committed that name to Coach Strauss and the Coyotes.

The last thing I need is to crush on Coach's untouchable daughter.

"You wanted to see me, Coach?" I walk into Coach Strauss's office after a grueling day at camp. My body aches, soreness wrapping around my quads and shooting all the way down my legs. And I'm famished.

But Callaway told me Coach wanted a word before I head out for the night, and while my initial response was confusion, I'm now concerned.

Did Leni tell him about running into me at the pool? Does he think our grabbing an ice cream is more than what it is? Is he going to warn me to stay away from his daughter?

This is why I don't do this shit. There's no time for distractions. Or confusion about where my loyalty lies. There's the team and that's it.

"Ah, Miller. Come on in." Coach beckons to the chair in front of his desk.

I sink into it and nearly wince as my body aches from the movement.

"I know you're probably eager to get home," Coach starts. I don't respond and the corner of his mouth twitches. He clasps his hands together and continues, "Leni mentioned seeing you at the pool the other night."

"Yeah. Stevens wants me to work more pool time into my conditioning."

"Right." Coach sighs and leans back in his chair.

Shit. He's pissed that I took Leni for an ice cream cone. That's what this is about, isn't it?

"Listen, I don't feel right asking you this. But truthfully, I don't know who else to ask. I guess Avery would do it but that could become its own fucking liability…" Coach mutters, partially to himself.

I frown, my body tensing. Are one of my teammates in trouble? Did something happen?

"My daughter's not herself lately," Coach says, staring right at me. His blue eyes are the same shade as Leni's, but they hold a hardness, degrees of wisdom, that his daughter doesn't yet possess. "The truth is, she hasn't been herself for a while." He blinks, looking exhausted. "Vicki and I are thrilled she's home. She's finding her footing, sorting out what comes next."

He pauses and I dip my chin, encouraging him to continue.

What's the ask?

"And she's back with her best friend from childhood, Marlowe, who is like a third daughter to me."

"Yeah," I say, recalling a few stories that Coach shared.

"Marlowe's boyfriend's parents have a lake house outside of Knoxville and Marlowe celebrates her birthday there for a weekend every summer. Vicki and I aren't too crazy about Leni going." He snorts. "And fortunately, she was away the past couple years."

I frown. "Coach, she's an adult." I point out the obvious. I mean, she's gotta be twenty-three, twenty-four years old. Hardly a high schooler looking to drink underage and skinny-dip with boys.

Coach swears softly. "I know." He looks at me miserably. "But there's something about this group of kids, this weekend… I don't trust it, Miller. One day, if you become a parent, you'll get what I'm saying. Call it father's intuition… but I don't want Leni going to Norris Lake on her own, with a bunch of peers who haven't seen her in years, except for Marlowe. And Marlowe's got her own stuff going on…" He trails off.

I hunch forward in my chair.

"What are you asking me, Coach?"

"Christ." He sighs again. "What am I asking you?" He raps his knuckles against the side of his desk. Then, he fixes me with a steely look. "Talon, I know it's unconventional and the timing is fucked. But in a few weeks, between our second and third preseason games, you've got a day off."

I nod, feeling my throat close as I know my day off is about to get axed.

"I would really appreciate it if you'd accompany Leni to Norris Lake that weekend." Coach lays it out, his lips pressed together as if it cost him something to ask me that.

And hell, it probably did. He's a proud man and not used to asking for favors.

But he's probably one of the only men I'd do anything for, no questions asked. Not because I owe him—which I do—but because I admire him so damn much. The way he shows up for others is the type of man I want to become.

Hell, he's the father figure I always wanted and never had —until I met him.

And now, he's giving me a chance to do something for his family after he did a hell of a lot for mine.

"Hell—" he swears. "Forget—"

"I'll go," I cut him off.

He freezes, watching me closely.

I lean forward in my chair. "Listen, I don't know Leni well. Two conversations and everything else is what you told me. But I think she's cool and if it puts your and Vicki's minds at ease that I hit up some birthday party with her…" I shrug in my chair. "I'll go."

Relief washes over Coach's face. "Thank you, Talon. I hate asking but—"

"Don't. I'm happy to do it. Really," I assure him.

"Okay." He nods. "They're heading up the third Friday in August so if you can get a morning workout in, I'll give you another day off."

Two days off. My body nearly weeps at the thought of extra recovery time. "I'll get the workout in."

"I know you will," Coach says.

"Um, does Leni know?" I ask.

Coach snorts before shaking his head. "No, not yet."

"Is that going to be a problem?" I can't imagine a woman being cool with her dad assigning her a chaperone for a weekend with her friends…but I don't get most family bonds. I never had any that mattered. While a part of me thinks it's ridiculous, a larger part thinks Coach's concern is sweet. Caring. Loving.

"Probably," Coach admits. "But I'll handle Leni."

I chuckle. "Maybe I can help." I gesture toward his phone. "Give me Leni's number. If you're sending me away for a weekend with her, we should at least grab a burger and talk."

Coach snaps his finger before pointing at me. "Great idea, Talon. Maybe tomorrow night? It can take some of the sting out when Vicki tells her you're tagging along."

I laugh. "Handling it, are you?"

Coach chuckles. "I'll send you her number. Thanks for doing this; I really appreciate it. Hell, maybe a weekend at the lake will help her snap out of the fog she's been in since she got home from New York. At this point, something's gotta give."

"Sure," I agree, not really understanding what he's talking about but knowing it doesn't fully pertain to me. Coach is a stand-up guy and a hell of a coach. But as a parent, his girls have got him wrapped around their manicured fingers. "Anything else?"

"That's it."

I stand to go when he stops me.

"Miller?"

"Yeah?" I turn around, stalling by the door to his office.

"I appreciate this, and I know I can trust you." His eyes harden and I work a swallow.

"Of course," I manage to say.

"But don't get any ideas. Leni doesn't date football players."

I dip my chin in understanding before I head out of his office.

And while I know it's true—my teammates have said as much—it still stings knowing Coach includes me in that group. Because while I know Leni Strauss is lightyears out of my league, I hate that Coach knows it too.

"A chaperone?!" I holler.

"Think of it like a buddy," Dad says soothingly, his palms outstretched like he's trying to calm a crazy, rabid wildebeest. Which, right now, is not too far off the mark.

"What is this, the eighteen hundreds?" I clap back.

"You haven't been with this group in a long time," Mom tries.

"Are you kidding me? I've known them all since high school. Hell, some of them since middle school. And I'm an adult. I'm twenty-four! I lived in Manhattan and took the subway and stayed out until sunrise just a year ago." I wave my arms emphatically.

God, I'm angry. But also…it feels good—normal—to feel something other than…shame. Emptiness. So, I lean into my anger and brandish my hands once more for good measure.

"But now you're back here," Dad reminds me, the gentleness gone. "My house—"

"Maybe I should move out," I interject.

Dad swears. Mom sighs. And I stew.

But I can't believe my dad asked one of his players to crash Marlowe's birthday weekend and be my fucking babysitter. How embarrassing is that?

Plus… "Don't you think you're crossing other lines?" I ask Dad.

He lifts an eyebrow, waiting for me to finish that thought.

"One of your players? A weekend away with your daughter?" I point to my chest. "What happened to no dating athletes?"

"Talon would never—" Dad starts.

"It's Talon Miller?" I shriek. Somehow, this is infinitely worse.

If it was Avery or Cohen, it would truly be like a brother looking out for his sister. Maybe Cohen would even have Raia come along and then it would just be…fun. Awkward, but fun.

Same with Leo Quincy. He would probably orchestrate birthday activities and time us in flip cup or something.

But…Talon Miller? Sexy, distracting, charismatic Talon Miller who seems to see more than what I'm projecting? Who took me for ice cream and made me laugh? Who makes me feel things I have no right feeling?

That's who my dad picked to babysit me?

"What is wrong with you?" I press.

Dad swears again, more colorfully this time. Then, he tosses his hands in the air and leaves the living room. A second later, the back door closes and I lean against the sofa, crossing my arms over my chest and glaring at Mom.

She takes a sip of her tea. "He's worried about you; we both are."

"I'm fine," I say defiantly.

Mom tilts her head, giving me a look. She knows I'm lying but won't call me on it because she's letting me have my pride. For this moment anyway.

I sigh and run my fingers over my eyebrows. "I'm fine," I say again, softer this time.

"I know you are. At least, you will be," Mom concedes. "Put our minds at ease and bring Talon to the party. No one will care. I bet Marlowe will be thrilled."

She will be; Mom knows her too well.

"Plus, did you ever think Talon wants to come?" Mom continues.

I give her a look.

"It's an extra day off for him to have some fun and relax. Swim in a lake and drink a beer. He's been putting in a lot of extra sessions. Maybe it will be good for him to have a break too."

I roll my eyes, not wanting to see her point. Besides, the whole arrangement is entirely unconventional. Not to mention unethical. The coach is giving a player an extra day off during preseason so he can chaperone his daughter's weekend plans?

Before I can toss back a retort, my phone buzzes with an incoming message and my stomach dips.

I pray that it's not Craig. I haven't heard from him in a few days and the distance is starting to feel normal. Healthy.

> Unknown Number: Hey Sunny Leni, it's Talon. You free for dinner?

My heart rate ticks up before I bite my bottom lip, embarrassment flooding through me as I realize my father put him up to this.

The man who never wanted me to date a player is now setting me up for a weekend with his star kicker. Not to date me of course, but to keep an eye on me.

The whole arrangement is messed up.

Gripping my phone, I stomp from the living room and blink back the tears in my eyes. This is such a fucking disaster.

In the safety of my bedroom, I slam my door closed and sink to the edge of my bed. Dragging a hand across my eyes, I suck in a breath and read Talon's message again.

A pity dinner date. *Ugh, could I be any more of a loser?*

My thumb hovers over the keyboard but I don't know

what to type back. I'm humiliated and frustrated. What do I say to save face?

Before I respond, another message appears.

Unknown Number: I'm craving tacos. Please don't leave me hanging.

I can't help the smile that tugs on the corners of my mouth. He's funny too. He doesn't take himself too seriously and I like that about him.

Sighing, I save him in my phone and tap out a reply.

Me: Alberto's?

Talon: Is there anywhere else to eat a taco on a Tuesday?

Me: I'm free.

Talon: I'll pick you up in thirty.

I confirm by giving his message a thumbs-up. Then, I hug my phone to my chest and drop backward onto my bed. Staring up at the ceiling, I try to regulate my breathing.

This isn't a date.

It's nothing. Just…tacos with a football star.

No big deal.

Mom knocks softly on my bedroom door and I sit up just as she enters.

"Leni," she says, her expression filled with understanding.

"Talon's picking me up for tacos," I say before she can add anything else.

Her eyes widen and she smiles. "He is? Well, isn't that lovely?"

I snort and shake my head, fighting my grin. I'm not sure when "lovely" became Mom's go-to word but she certainly uses it to temper my emotions.

Mom catches my almost-smile. "It is," she decides, nodding. "I'll let you get ready then." She backs out of my room and closes the door with a soft snick.

Shit! I need to get ready.

Rushing from my bed, I tug open my closet and flip through the hangers. Alberto's is a low-key taco and tequila kind of spot. And yet, I don't want to wear cut-off shorts and a T-shirt. But I don't want to look overdressed either since this dinner date is…nothing.

Biting the corner of my lip, I finally settle on a simple, royal blue maxi dress and gold strappy sandals. I pull my hair back into a low ponytail, apply a minimal amount of makeup, and add some gold hoop earrings. It's elevated summer casual. I could have come from shopping with Mom.

Pleased with my appearance, I grab a small crossbody purse, stuff my phone and some cash inside, and relocate to the living room.

Relief floods my veins when I spot the note from Mom.

Leni—I took Dad out for dinner! Have fun tonight. Love you, Mom

My mom is the best. I know she got Dad out of the house to save me any more embarrassment. At least now, I won't have to suffer through Dad and Talon having some awkward exchange about me riding in his car to Alberto's.

I wait for Talon in the living room and pull my phone out to randomly scroll through social media when a message comes through, stopping me cold.

> Craig: Leni, are you ready to talk yet?

My heart rate accelerates at seeing his name. I read his message several times, as if there's a hidden meaning. Is there?

> Craig: You can't avoid me forever, sweetheart. I know we argued but moving out was a mistake. Breaking up was a mistake.

Tears prick the corners of my eyes as my stomach bottoms out and my heart rushes upward into my throat. My hands begin to shake and the words on the screen swim in front of my eyes.

I should block his number. Hell, I've tried to block him. But there's something about cutting Craig off completely that terrifies me. If I end the channel of communication, will he come for me? If so, I won't have any warning. I won't suspect it at all. Somehow, receiving Craig's messages, being able to assess his mental state, offers a glimmer of reassurance that he's in New York and not here.

But will he ever move on? Or has my taking a stand become a new challenge for Craig?

Blinking rapidly, I manage to avoid crying.

Outside, a car door closes.

I blink faster, running one palm along the length of my dress.

Why is Craig doing this to me now? Why is he swooping back in right as I'm about to take a step forward?

Nerves skitter through my limbs and a shiver runs down my spine. My thumb hovers over the keyboard of my phone.

If I finally reply, and tell him again that it's over, will that shut him down for good? Or encourage him to show up in person?

> Craig: I need you, baby. Give me the chance to fight for us. Call me.

"Jesus," I murmur, shocked by his admission.

I need you.

Does he? Can I help him seek help?

No! I shake my head at my thoughts.

The pad of my thumb runs over his name on screen, and I can hear his voice in my mind.

I love you, Leni. I'm gonna make you my wife one day.

I believed him.

I rub the inside of my left wrist, a phantom pain blossoming. Before I can fully recall that night, the doorbell rings and I jump up. My phone falls to the floor, and I swear, bending down to retrieve it.

I clench my hand into a fist to stop the trembling of my fingers.

Get it together, Strauss.

Mentally pep-talking myself, I stash my phone in my purse, straighten my shoulders, and stride to the door. Pulling it open, I'm rendered speechless as Talon turns to face me on the front porch.

He's wearing light-washed jeans, Nike sneakers, and a paper thin, heather gray V-neck T-shirt. He looks relaxed and comfortable. Confident and gorgeous.

"Hey, Len." He grins.

"H-hi, Talon," I sputter, my voice shaking slightly. My grip tightens on my purse.

His eyebrows pull together. "You okay?"

I clear my throat. "Yeah. Yes," I amend, a forced laugh escaping my throat. I settle the strap of my purse over my shoulder. Against my hip, I feel my phone vibrate with an incoming message.

It takes everything in me not to check it. *Is it Craig?* Deep down, I know it is. And I know that even though he hasn't snapped yet, he's getting close to losing it since I haven't replied to any of his messages. He'll know that I'm keeping him on read status and it'll be a blow to his ego.

A month ago, I wouldn't dare not answer.

But right now, with Talon standing before me looking

somewhat confused and concerned, I force myself to step onto the porch, lock the front door, and push Craig as far from my mind as I can.

Which, admittedly, isn't very far. But it's a hell of a lot farther than it was a week ago.

And that's progress.

6
TALON

She's nervous.

As I follow her to my ride, I take in the rigidity of her posture. The clasp she keeps on her purse. Twice she reaches for the side of her neck as if searching for…what?

Is she nervous about spending time with me? Is she angry with Coach? Is it something else?

I can't tell. But her reaction is unsettling and I don't know what the hell to do about it. I'm going to spend an entire weekend with this woman in two and a half weeks' time and I don't know a damn thing about her. Except that, despite her being easy to talk to, she's more difficult to get a read on than any other woman I've hung out with.

She's both warm and reserved. Quirky and disciplined. Sweet and standoffish. The woman she is when we're in the swimming pool—just the two of us—is different than the anxious version that emerges once a crowd forms, like in the bustling ice cream shop. I catch glimpses of two Lenis—one version echoes everything Coach shared about her and one is at odds with Coach's stories.

My daughter's not herself lately.

Knowing that Coach and Vicki are worried about Leni triggers my concern for her.

Leni slides into the passenger seat of my SUV and I round

the front, slipping behind the wheel. I gaze over at her as I turn on the engine. "You sure you're good?"

She clicks in her seat belt before meeting my gaze. Her smile is tight and her eyes—so damn blue—are guarded. "Yeah. Yes. I'm fine."

I lift a skeptical eyebrow.

"I love Alberto's," she chatters, clearly wanting to change the subject.

Sighing, I back out of Coach's driveway and point my SUV toward the main road. "It's a good spot. You've been hitting it for years?"

"Since high school," she confirms.

"Did you miss it here? When you were in New York?" I ask, trying to keep a conversation going. When we went out for ice cream, it was easy but something about tonight is off and I have no clue what the hell it is.

This is why I don't do this shit. Women are complicated and that means more distractions. I'm not the type of guy who tries to figure out women's moods. I keep my shit light. Fleeting. Temporary.

And I really don't have any female friendships to speak of either so it's not like I possess any insight into the inner workings of a woman's mind. I'm happier being on the outside. At least, I used to be.

I'd be lying if I said Leni doesn't fascinate me.

"I did," she says on a sigh. And it sounds like the weight of the world whooshes out of her on that exhale.

"That why you came home?" I press.

Her head snaps toward me and her eyes narrow. I glance at her, confused by her reaction.

"Yeah. Why else would I come home?" She sounds defensive.

I shrug. "Just trying to get to know you, Leni."

She sighs heavily again. "I know. I'm...I'm sorry, Talon. The truth is, I'm really embarrassed that my dad reached out

to you about Marlowe's birthday weekend. And I know this"
—she gestures between is—"is you feeling bad for me and—"

"I don't feel bad for you," I cut in.

She rears back slightly. "Really? This isn't some pity dinner offer?"

"No," I say, meaning it. "This is me really trying to get to know you so we can have fun at the lake instead of shit being awkward between us. You know what my lifestyle is like, Len. I don't get a lot of time off. If I get a free weekend at a lake house during the summer, I don't want to waste that shit. I want to enjoy it."

She rolls her lips together, weighing my words. "You want to go?"

"Sure. Why not?"

"And you're not mad my dad put you up to this?" She gestures toward herself like she's some pain in the ass nuisance. And a part of me hates that she thinks that about herself.

"Look," I say, hanging a right and pulling into the parking lot of Alberto's. "Your dad's done a lot for me. Professionally and personally. I'd say yeah, no questions asked, to almost anything he asks of me. But hanging with you for a weekend, swimming in a lake, drinking a beer? It's hardly a hardship, Leni." I park my SUV, flip the ignition, and turn to look at her. "Now, can we please cut this weird awkward shit and eat some tacos? I'd prefer to go into the weekend as friends."

"Friends," she repeats, as if testing out the word. I can't tell if she's relieved or disappointed by the label, but it's the best I can do. I mean, yeah, she's gorgeous and sweet and if I met her somewhere other than Knoxville, I'd probably try to get in her pants.

But she's Coach's kid. I'm about to start the season. And I know better than to shit where I eat.

So… "Friends," I confirm.

She grins and it's the first real smile she's given me all night. "I'd like that."

"Good. Now come on. Today was brutal and I'm fucking starving." I push open the driver's side door.

Leni meets me at the back of my SUV and we walk into Alberto's together. It's hopping, with nearly full tables and pockets of loud conversations. The walls are bright, with colorful calavera paintings decorating the space.

An empty high-top table sits off to the side and I hope Leni and I can snag it before a group from the bar relocates.

"Oh my God!" a woman shrieks, waving at us. "Leni! I didn't know you were coming here for dinner!" Her eyes dart to me and her mouth drops open. "Holy shit! Is that Talon Miller?"

Beside me, Leni straightens, her body on alert. All that stress that seeped from her on the ride over gathers once more, causing her shoulder blades to nearly touch.

I place a hand on her lower back in an attempt to soothe her. She flinches and I drop my hand immediately. Her eyes snap to mine, horror filling them.

"Sorry," we say in unison.

I shake my head. "I'm sorry," I bite out the words, completely out of my element. I obviously made her uncomfortable. What the hell do I do now?

"Join us!" The woman rushes forward. She throws her arms around Leni, hugging her hard, before facing me. "Hi! I'm Marlowe."

"The birthday girl," I say, putting two and two together.

Marlowe beams. "Yes!" she squeals, her eyes widening as she bounces up onto her toes. "Do you want to come to my party?"

Finding my footing, I manage an easy smirk. "Can't wait. Leni invited me."

"Leni!" Marlowe shrieks again. God, she's loud. Or, I narrow my eyes, a little drunk. "You didn't tell me."

"I hope that's okay," Leni says.

Her friend frowns. "Of course, it's okay." She laughs. "Are you crazy?" She glances at me again. "I'd love for you to join, Talon."

"Thanks," I say, my attention snagging on the guy stepping up behind Marlowe. He looks the opposite of happy at this news.

"Babe," Marlowe gushes, grabbing his forearm. "Leni is bringing Talon to the lake house. Isn't that great?"

"Hey, Toby." Leni lifts a hand in a halfhearted wave.

"You dating football players now, Len?" Toby asks, ignoring me. His eyes narrow on Leni as if she owes him an explanation.

What the hell is that about?

I widen my stance, crossing my arms over my chest. I know I'm not for everyone, but this dude doesn't even know me. To flat out ignore me is...fucking odd. I hold a hand out anyway, trying to take the higher road. "Talon."

He stares at my hand for a beat before shaking it. Weak-ass grip. "Toby."

"This is my boyfriend." Marlowe bounces again. Definitely tipsy.

"Well, I'm looking forward to your party," I tell her. "We're going to grab a bite."

"You should sit with us," Marlowe continues, pointing to a back table where another guy is seated. This guy waves easily and Leni grins, waving back.

While the second dude seems cool, I'm not really interested in having a group dinner with strangers.

I want to get to know Leni, who is confounding me with each passing second.

Marlowe continues to gush, and Toby's scowl deepens. I frown, trying to get a read on their dynamic. It's fucking weird.

"Oh my God! Is this a date?" Marlowe asks, her gaze

darting between Leni and me. I amend my earlier observation. She not tipsy; she's drunk. That flat-out question can't be part of girl code.

Deciding I don't want to be part of this conversation a second longer, I reach for Leni's hand. "Too early to tell, Marlowe. We're going to grab a table but see you soon, yeah?"

"Oh yes. Of course!" She grabs Leni's other arm and does some weird girl shriek and arm flapping. "Call me later, Leni."

"I will," Leni promises.

Toby says nothing. In fact, he sneers at Leni, almost like he's mad that she's here.

I flag down a server and we're seated at the high-top table. Leni reaches for a menu.

"What was that about?" I ask, flipping my chin in the direction of Toby.

"What?" Leni follows my line of sight. "Oh, that's just Toby."

"He's kind of a douche."

Her eyes widen and a snort of laughter erupts. "He is." She nods. "He's a huge douche." She shakes her head. "But Marlowe's my best friend so…"

"You play nice."

"I try," Leni admits. "Her cousin Keller, the other guy at the table, is much better at it than I am. Most of the time, it takes everything I have not to lose my shit on Toby. Mar deserves so much better. They've been together since high school though—there's a lot of history there."

"Right," I say, reaching for a menu. But…there's something else there too. Something I can't put my finger on. And for the first time, I think Coach may be right. I can't call it father's intuition, but I wouldn't want Leni spending solo time at a lake house with a guy like that either.

So, it's a good thing I'm going.

7

Leni

"WHAT'S YOUR FAVORITE COLOR?" I ASK AFTER TAKING A LONG pull of my Diet Coke. I ease back in my seat, smiling as Talon takes a swig of his Coke.

When he ordered it—and didn't opt for a beer, the way Toby always does or a scotch, the way Craig always did—tension drained from my shoulders. Tension I didn't realize I was carrying until that moment.

"Blue. You?"

"Green," I admit.

"What's your favorite band?" he wonders.

"The Burnt Clovers," I reply.

He chuckles. "You know West has an in with them, right?"

"Stop!" I nearly gush, frowning as an old memory filters through my mind. "I know Derek Reiner was at the Super Bowl but…" I trail off, trying to recall the rest of the story Dad —or was it Lincoln?—shared.

"Yeah. Nova's best friends with his girlfriend, Allegra."

I snap my fingers and point toward Talon as it clicks. "That's right. Lincoln told me that."

"They play in Tennessee sometimes," he continues.

I nod. "I'll remember that. I'd love to see them live."

"I haven't been to many concerts," Talon admits.

"Really?" I lean forward. "Lincoln and I went on a trip to Ireland a few summers ago. There was live music everywhere, spilling out of pubs and onto the streets. It was wonderful," I sigh, recalling the ease of that summer. The simplicity and the freedom and the being. Enjoying with no strings attached or expectations woven through it.

I haven't felt like that in a long, long time. The memory of that trip makes me miss my sister. When I put space between myself and my friends and family, I nearly cut Lincoln off.

Not because I wanted to but because deep down, I knew that she'd figure it out. She always was smarter than me.

"Ireland," Talon murmurs, pulling me back to the conversation. He squints. "I think my mom was Irish. Or maybe Scottish."

"You think?" I blurt out, before I realize how rude I sound.

Talon shrugs one arm, brushing it off. "I was brought up in the system."

I frown, trying to understand his words. "Like, foster care?" I ask slowly.

"Yeah," he admits. "Like foster care."

My chest squeezes tightly as I realize I don't know much about Talon. Where were his parents? What happened to his family? "For how long?" I ask instead.

"From when I was three until I aged out."

"At eighteen?" I confirm, mentally doing the math. Fifteen years.

For fifteen years, Talon was in foster care. Was he with one family? Does he have foster brothers and sisters he keeps in touch with? He doesn't offer any more information and I don't know how to ask.

Talon nods. Whatever he reads in my expression has him reaching over the table and tugging my wrist. "Don't feel bad for me, Sunny Leni. It wasn't all bad."

"I'm…I'm not." I hate when someone gives me their pity or compassion. I hate when people try to relate to my breakup with Craig when they have no idea what it entails. The breakup was the tip of the iceberg—and the portion below the surface was massive and wildly perilous. The last thing I want is for Talon to think I'm pitying him. Or worse, judging.

"I found football," he continues, and I know he doesn't believe me. His thumb drags across the skin just above my wrist and it feels nice. Safe. Not a precursor to a pinch. "I found a family in my team."

"My dad," I mutter.

"Your dad's done a lot for me," he reminds me.

"Do you keep in touch with any of your foster family members?" I ask, trying to understand.

Talon shakes his head, his lips pinched into a smirk that doesn't reach his eyes.

I clear my throat, wondering how Talon navigated life for so long, found success, without family to guide him. My family has comprised my entire foundation. And here I am, pushing them away.

"Don't pity me," Talon whispers.

I blink and smooth out my expression. "So you might be Irish," I say, trying to get the conversation back on track. The last thing I want to do is make Talon feel uncomfortable.

He laughs lightly, his eyes sparking with appreciation for my subject change. "Could be."

"You need to go to a concert," I decide.

Talon grins, his fingers closing around my wrist loosely. "And what? If I enjoy it, it means I'm Irish."

I shrug, laughing with him. "I don't know. It could be telling of your ancestry." My eyebrows lift. "Have you ever done one of those ancestry DNA tests? That could be—"

"No," Talon cuts me off, shaking his head. His laughter is gone and in its place is a seriousness I don't understand. "I've never done it." He tempers his tone.

I roll my lips together, my eyes silently asking the question I won't voice: *Why not?*

Talon sighs. He shakes his head and leans back in his chair, dropping his hold on my grip. A beat passes, and the conversations swirling around us in Alberto's grow louder as Talon remains quiet. Then, he leans forward and admits, "No one wanted me. After my mom… After my mom lost custody of me, no one came forward as next of kin. If I do the test and there's a match…a grandparent or an aunt or uncle…" Talon's voice trails off. "I've made peace with where I'm at. I don't want to go back and have to unpack things I've already laid to rest."

His tone is hard but his words drip with an honesty, a vulnerability, that surprises me. I didn't think he'd elaborate further but he chose to share this deeply personal information with me.

What does that mean? This isn't just a football player doing my dad a solid. This is a man confiding in me…and now searching my eyes for what? Understanding? Acceptance?

This time it's me reaching across the table. I lace my fingers with Talon's and press our palms together, silently letting him know that I'm here for whatever he wants to share. "I'm sorry you missed out on what could have, or should have, been. And I'm sorry if I pried. I think you're amazing, Talon."

He scoffs and I tighten my hold.

"I wish I could be brave enough to talk about the things I'm trying to lay to rest."

His eyes narrow at that and a muscle in his jaw tics.

"Thank you for taking me out tonight," I say, infusing my tone with my sincerity. This is a hell of a lot more than just dinner. For me, this is another step forward that I never thought I'd take. Talon elevating our conversation beyond surface level, him trusting me in a way I don't deserve, heals some of the wounds Craig inflicted.

I'm not a failure at everything. In some things, I am enough.

Talon dips his head and clears his throat. Then, he tilts his chin toward our approaching server. "Here come our tacos. What's at the top of your bucket list?"

I bite my bottom lip, knowing our conversation was heading into uncharted waters and right now, we need some levity. "Thank you." I grin at the server when she sets down our plates.

Talon takes a big bite of his taco and groans appreciatively.

"It's the best here," I agree, taking a bite of mine. Perfect amount of spice. Fresh ingredients. *Chef's kiss.* "See the Northern Lights," I answer his question.

Talon looks up. "The Northern Lights? Like, when the sky changes colors?"

"Yeah," I say, chewing another bite of taco. "There's places above the Arctic Circle where you can stay in an igloo or dome bubble and see the Northern Lights." I lean closer as excitement fills my veins. I've always wanted to see the most spectacular light show on Earth. When I told Craig my desire to see the Aurora Borealis, he rolled his eyes and commented that I sound like a girl who never had to work for my own experiences. But Talon's looking at me with interest—maybe a bit of awe—in his irises. "You can access these hotels by reindeer-pulled sleighs or snowmobiles. You can even go skiing or wear snowshoes. And at night, you look right through the ceiling and stare up at the sky and just…take it all in. I'd love to see that."

"Wow," Talon breathes, his eyes steadfast on mine. "I—I didn't know that even existed."

I nod, taking another bite of my taco. "I think that would be incredible."

Talon nods. "I've never met anyone like you, Leni," he says, surprising me.

For a beat, I wonder if that's good or bad.

"You like your tacos?" Talon asks, changing the topic again.

"They're great," I admit. Our conversation continues, naturally and organically. In fact, with a new thread of trust connecting us, it feels more like a date than two friends grabbing a bite.

It feels like the new beginning I crave.

We order dessert, share funny stories, and talk about the team and Knoxville.

Talon drops me off at Mom and Dad's and wishes me good night with a raised hand and a crooked smile.

I bite my bottom lip when I ascend the porch steps and turn to give him a little wave before I enter the house. Part of me feels like I'm floating, the time spent with Talon making me giddy.

My parents are already asleep so I get ready for bed. When I climb beneath the covers and check my phone, Craig's messages appear. For a handful of hours, I nearly forgot about them. About him.

At the reminder, a coldness sweeps through my limbs, replacing the warmth my evening with Talon provided.

Craig: I'm not going to wait forever, Leni.

Craig: You know I'm not a patient man.

Craig: But for you, I'm trying.

Craig: We belong together, Leni. I won't just let you go.

Shaking my head, I place my phone screen-down and don't bother replying. Tonight was good and I'm proud of myself for not allowing Craig to ruin in.

Instead, I go to bed feeling more fulfilled, lighter, than I have in ages.

Right before I doze off, I realize I never asked Talon about the top of his bucket list. Or if he has one at all.

"And Mr. Stanson will do the opening remarks," Marylee shares as the other ladies look down at the their binders, taking notes.

"What about Mr. McIntyre?" Anna Louise asks.

Silence settles over the group. I sit up straighter, my curiosity piqued at the mention of Marlowe's grandfather.

Marylee glances around the group before lowering her voice. "He's not attending."

Sarah Gilbert gasps.

Margaret Jeffries shakes her head, looking disgusted. "Because of the scandal."

Scandal? I look at Mom. She looks just as bewildered as I feel.

Marlowe didn't tell me about a scandal…

Mom leans closer and, like a gust of wind, my body follows suit.

"His granddaughter—" Marylee starts.

"Marlowe?" Mom wonders.

"Adeline," Anna Louise clarifies. Marlowe's younger sister.

"Caught him putting his hands on Samantha," Marylee continues.

"That's his third wife." Anna Louise glances at Mom and me to catch us up to speed. But of course, I already know that. Marlowe was horrified when her grandfather married Samantha, a woman "only eight years old than me!" Marlowe had cried.

Mom's body slouches, as if the news is a physical blow. But it is. It always is.

And for me, I feel it right through my chest. My fingers absently reach for the side of my neck, graze along my collarbone.

Craig's ignored text messages flicker through my mind. Oh, but he must be reeling with anger.

Grandpa McIntyre hit his wife. I shake my head in disbelief, recalling all the dinners I had in his home.

Why didn't Marlowe tell me?

"Mr. Stanson pushed him out," Sarah offers, albeit uncertainly.

"And a good fucking riddance," Anna Louise declares, not looking the least big chagrined for her foul language.

Not that she should. No one should.

Mr. McIntyre hit his sweet young wife and Adeline saw.

Knots tighten in my stomach and nausea rolls up into my throat.

I clasp my hands in my lap, as if pressing my palms together will somehow keep me from coming apart at the seams.

"Will Adeline still attend?" Mom whispers, most likely hoping she isn't being punished for her grandfather's fuckup.

"I didn't realize Adi received an invitation," I murmur.

Marylee smiles gently. "You've been gone a long time, Leni."

Beside me, Mom reaches for my hand and I let her take it. Things are different now.

"Old McIntyre wanted to ship her off to boarding school immediately after the incident, but Marlowe put her foot down." Anna Louise bangs the end of her fist against the table to punctuate her words.

"Anna Louise," Sarah says gently.

"Sorry." Anna Louise doesn't look the least bit sorry.

"Marlowe intervened?" I ask, wondering why my friend didn't tell me...any of this.

Like you've been honest with her?

I shake the hard truth out of my mind.

"Sure did. She's been taking Adeline to the dance rehearsals herself," Marylee confirms.

"She's a good sister," Sarah remarks.

"What about—" I start to ask about Marlowe's mother, but Mom squeezes my fingers and I swallow back the rest of my question. We're talking about things no one speaks of in the openness of the club.

At least, not without martinis in hand.

Marylee glances at me, her eyes brimming with sadness.

How many women here have suffered at the hands of our boyfriends, husbands, or relatives? I glance around the table and hate the heaviness that hangs over it. Over us.

Because we all know someone. And in my case...my throat tightens and I curl my fingernails into my palms.

Marylee clears her throat. "Mr. Stanson will do the opening remarks."

"Right," Sarah agrees.

And we get back on track with the meeting. With the planned ceremony of events.

With talking about floral arrangements and table linens.

But a stone lands heavily in my stomach and stays there for the rest of the day.

It weighs down my limbs and clouds my mind. So much so that after the long meeting and lunch with the ladies, I change into my swimsuit, pack a bag, and head to the pool.

When I leave the locker room and approach the swimming lanes, two gray-green eyes meet mine and I smile.

For the first time all day, some of the pressure eases. Some of the guilt of not knowing what Marlowe's been managing lessens.

Talon Miller grins and my heart skips a damn beat.

"Hey there, Sunny Leni," he calls out, leaning against the edge of the swimming pool like he's relaxing on a sofa.

"Fancy seeing you here," I say, drawing closer.

I sit on the ledge, the pool water lapping at my toes.

Talon smirks. "I'm hardly fancy." He says it jokingly, but I note the seriousness in his eyes.

He's laid-back, casual, and familiar. Charismatic and fun.

And yet, his tone speaks to a regret. Or, worse, an apology.

"Fancy is overrated." I shrug, my thoughts still caught up on Grandpa McIntyre.

He cocks his head, looking up at me. "Is it?" he murmurs, before reaching for my hand.

Before I can sort out the meaning behind his words, he tugs me forward and I half fall, half jump into the pool.

"Talon!" I snort, shaking water from my eyes and smacking his shoulder.

"You need to warm up, Leni?"

"Warm up?" I sputter. "For what?"

"You ready to race?"

"You?" I laugh, shaking my head. "You don't stand a chance, Miller."

He grins, flexing his muscles obnoxiously. Deliciously. "Care to back up that claim?"

I grip the side of the wall, curiosity piqued. "What are you suggesting?"

"A friendly wager." His eyes glisten.

"How friendly?" Mine narrow.

And oh, do his spark. "If I win, you let me take you out tomorrow night."

My heart rate doubles at his words.

Is this another friend date? To prepare for our weekend together?

Or…is this different? More.

My legs kick the water beneath me. Hope rises in my chest and I suck in a breath to temper it.

Talon quirks an eyebrow…waiting.

I clear my throat. "And when I win—"

He laughs at my word choice and tugs on the end of my ponytail. "I'll let you pick the restaurant." He passes me my swim cap. "Get ready, Sunny Leni. We race in ten."

"What?" I shake my head.

"Nine," Talon begins to count.

Rushing, I pull on my swim cap and snap my goggles into place.

"Three, Two—" He lowers his goggles and we both get into position. "One. Go!"

I push off the wall and swim as hard as I can. But I'm not desperate to beat Talon Miller. Either way, I win.

Because it means another evening spent with him.

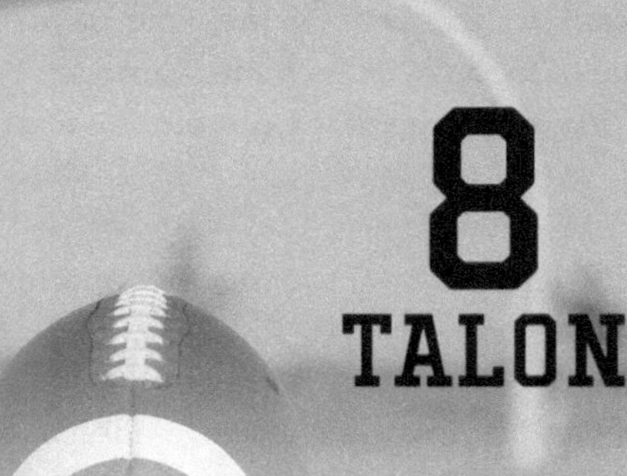

8
TALON

"YOU CHEATED!" I ACCUSE AS I HIT THE WALL A STROKE behind her.

She laughs. "Don't let Freddy hear you say that. Those are fighting words."

"Freddy?" I shake my head, pulling off my goggles.

Leni blushes. "It's what my friends call Dad," she admits.

My eyebrows lift. "Freddy?" I sputter, unable to see Coach Strauss as anything other than Coach.

Leni giggles, lifting her hand to her mouth sweetly. Innocently.

God, but she's cute.

Stop flirting with her!

But I can't because being with Leni, talking and joking and hanging with her, is the most natural I've ever felt around a woman. Things with her are...easy. Sometimes, alarmingly so. I find myself sharing things with her that my closest teammates don't know.

"I beat you fair and square," she says, pushing her index finger into my chest.

Reaching over the lane divider, I tug her closer. "Fair and square?" I repeat. "Who says things like that?"

She blushes again, deeper this time. Like she's actually embarrassed. "I do," is her retort.

I snort and shake my head. "You do," I agree. "I'll take

you anywhere you want to go, Len. Name your favorite restaurant. Favorite type of food. Whatever you want."

She ponders this for a moment. "Do you have any allergies?"

"Nope," I admit.

"Do you live alone?" Her eyebrows tug together and for a beat, I can't read her expression.

"I do."

She sucks in a breath and stares at me for several seconds, a faint blush warming her cheeks.

I wait for her to continue, searching her expression for a clue about what she's going to say. My gaze drops to her lips and I instantly regret it. Leni's lips are slightly parted and soft pink—practically begging to be kissed.

"My favorite meal is schnitzel. It's my grandmother's recipe and one of the only dishes I make pretty well." She bites her bottom lip, as if unsure, and I force myself to blink. "I can make it for us. But—"

"You want to cook dinner for me?" I interrupt, feeling a kick behind my breastbone. No one's ever cooked for me before. I mean, other than the various foster parents I collected over the years—who mostly did the bare minimum to ensure I was fed—and some team dinners sponsored by a coach or a teammate's parents. But not counting myself, there's been no one who has ever made a meal specifically for me.

Leni tugs off her swim cap and clenches it in her fist. Her hair tumbles down, framing her face and draping over her shoulders.

She steels her shoulders and clears her throat, as if shoring up her resolve. "Yes. I'd like to cook for you, Talon."

I nearly drown in her eyes. My gaze darts between them as if trying to find a hidden motive. Or…something.

Because why would this woman who is lightyears out of

my league want to do something…nice for me? Especially after she won the race. The wager.

"Can you come over at seven?" My voice is deeper than it was a minute ago.

Leni nods solemnly.

A moment passes between us and I don't know how to shut this down. This is more than flirtation. We're veering into dangerous territory.

I clear my throat and Leni breaks eye contact, glancing down.

"Send me a list of ingredients and—"

"I'll bring everything I need," she says.

"Please, Len," I mutter, needing to contribute something to one of the kindest gestures I've ever received. I've never had a woman be so…thoughtful toward me. "Send me a list and I'll get the ingredients. Okay?"

She glances up, holds my gaze, and nods.

"Okay," I confirm, reaching out to brush a lock of hair behind her shoulder. I wrap the blonde strand around my index finger, studying the different shades of sunshine. Platinum and honey. Gold and champagne.

Shit. What am I doing? Touching her like this. Touching her at all.

"Okay," I breathe out again, sounding like a damn parrot. I tuck the strand behind her ear, my thumb brushing against her earlobe and pressing against her silver star stud earring. She sucks in a breath and involuntarily leans into my touch. As if she can't help herself, as if she wants me the same way I want her.

I force myself to drop my hand. Lower my gaze. I need to get out of here. I need to put space between us.

Heaving myself out of the pool, I shake off some of the water. "I better let you get your laps in," I mutter. "You have my number?" Stupid. I texted her first; of course she has my number.

Leni looks up at me, her eyes tracking up my frame. She bites her bottom lip and my cock stirs to life, my wet swim trunks leaving nothing to the imagination.

Leni's eyes drop to half-mast and it's a pure shot of lust. Want. Desire.

Dammit.

"I have your number," she confirms, a promise lingering in her tone.

I run a palm over my hair. I need to hit the locker room. "Then, I'll see you tomorrow, Sunny Leni."

"Seven p.m."

"At seven." I back away from her.

When I'm half a lane away, I force myself to turn around.

Then I shove my way into the locker room and suck in a gulp of oxygen.

I'm playing with fucking fire. And forget getting burned; I'm about to burn down everything I've ever worked for.

And still, I can't wait for dinner tomorrow night.

She wants to cook me dinner.

Callaway: Anyone up for a drink?

I lift an eyebrow, surprised our team captain would want to grab a beer with our second preseason game coming up.

Campbell: A drink?

I chime in for good measure.

Me: Like, a tea?

Quincy: I could go for an espresso.

> Gutierrez: You good, Callaway?

> Baglione: Quincy, you need a pastry for that espresso?

> Campbell: (laughing faces emoji)

> Quincy: (middle finger emoji)

> Callaway: Corks?

> Baglione: Womp. No espresso for Fancypants.

> Quincy: Fancypants was serious about the espresso. I'm grabbing one with Harper. See you tomorrow.

I snicker, knowing Leo will have a better conversation with one of his long-time friends, Harper Henderson. They go way back and most likely, Harper's boyfriend, NHL player Damien Barnes, will join.

> Baglione: I'm beat tonight. Sorry, bro.

> Gutierrez: My sister's in town. Taking her for dinner.

> Campbell: Don't get pissy—

> Callaway: Not one word about my sister.

I laugh louder. Cohen Campbell going after little Raia Callaway was a flea flicker no one saw coming. The fact that Callaway is cool with it is even more shocking. But I guess on some level, having your best friend, the guy you trust the most, date your sister isn't the worst thing in the world. At least Avery knows Cohen worships Raia and will always treat her like a treasure.

> Me: I'll meet you, Callaway.

Callaway: 20 minutes.

Me: See you there.

I place my phone on the kitchen island and move toward my bedroom. I change quickly, having already showered after the pool. Since I returned from swimming, I've been in a head fog, wondering how badly I'm messing up my future—my game—by tangling up with Leni. Even though it's innocent.

Nothing happened.

I mean, a few glances at her lips and now…dinner.

God, what am I thinking?

The only thing I have in my life is football. As the kicker, my mental focus is nearly paramount to my physical endurance. My skills on the field are largely connected to the headspace I cultivate.

And right now, with preseason games and intense media coverage, with the Coyotes making cuts left and right, it's imperative that I keep my head in the game. Literally.

All I can think about is Leni making me dinner tomorrow night. Schnitzel. A family recipe.

I didn't even know what the fuck a schnitzel was until I met the Strauss family. They're all cultured and well-traveled and I'm…trying to fucking survive and keep my position in the process.

Avery's message is a welcome distraction. Knowing that I can hang with him instead of alone in my condo is a reprieve I'm grateful for.

Tossing on shorts and a shirt, I slide into sandals and grab my wallet and keys. Then, I drive to Corks, post up at the bar, and order two beers.

Avery arrives a few minutes later, grinning when he sees me.

"Ballsy," he comments, jutting his chin toward the Heineken.

"We don't have to finish them," I admit, knowing he doesn't drink heavily during preseason. Hell, neither do I. But tonight…tonight I need the distraction of a cold beer too.

Avery chuckles and takes the stool next to mine.

"What's going on?" I ask.

He shrugs, taps his pint against mine, and takes a swig. "Honestly? I had to get out of my house."

I sigh. "Same."

Avery lifts an eyebrow. "I think I have a fucking stalker."

"What?" I snort, shaking my head as the beer I was about to swallow burns the back of my nose. "A stalker?"

"Fuck, bro," Avery groans.

"Is it the *Sports Illustrated* MILF?" I wonder, recalling an older woman Avery was hooking up with.

"No. This is even worse. She's one of Raia's teammate's sisters." He takes a swig of his beer, frowning. "Older sister, too."

"Huh?"

Avery shakes his head, looking confused. "She's gotta be twenty-six. Twenty-seven."

"Are you worried? Is she…threatening?"

"No, nothing like that." He waves a hand. "She came to a few of the open practices and…shit, I don't know. She must have gotten my address from her sister and…she's been fucking everywhere. Today, I'm certain I saw her in the lobby of my building. And then, again tonight, at the coffee shop on the corner by my place."

"That's strange."

"What's strange is she doesn't give off enamored, I-have-a-crush-on-an-athlete vibes. It's more like she's…curious. Or, conducting research or something."

"What do you mean?" I frown. I've never heard of a stalker like this.

"I feel like she's watching me, or interested, but it's…clinical somehow. I don't get the feeling that she's trying to hook-up or anything like that."

"Huh." I take a swig of my beer, speechless.

He shakes his head. "It's the weirdest thing. But she seems like a cool woman. I mean, she's harmless. The whole thing is just…different."

"Right."

"I just wanted out of my place." He tips his beer toward me. "What's your excuse?"

I shrug. "Just gotta get out of my head."

"What are you caught up on?"

"Leni Strauss," I admit.

Avery rears back, his expression morphing from one of nonchalance to downright concern. "Are you fucking kidding?" he hisses. "Coach's daughter!"

"It's not like that," I backpedal, mentally swearing at myself for being so goddamn careless. But she is at the fore-front of my mind and…I don't understand why. I don't get what the hell is transpiring between us. "Coach asked me to look out for her."

Avery's eyebrows pull together. "He did?"

"Yeah. And…she's a cool woman too, you know?"

"Yeah, I fucking know that." Avery watches me closely, as if he's reading between the lines. But there's nothing to read. I'm grappling, spilling my thoughts, as they pop into my mind.

I shrug. "She's a friend."

"A friend," Avery repeats.

I take a pull of my beer. I need to steer this conversation in a different direction. And fast. "But after meeting some of her friends, I get why Coach is worried."

Avery leans closer, as if pulled by the edge in my tone. "You think something's wrong?"

I bite my bottom lip, considering his words. "I don't know. But there's something there…something that isn't adding up." The way she looks like she's holding herself together. Her sudden return to Knoxville from New York—which Coach said was her dream when she first accepted an internship there. Her reaction to her best friend's boyfriend, Toby. And...the way I'm drawn to her. The protectiveness she evokes from me. "There's...something." I'm not making any damn sense.

Avery hangs his head, partially in defeat. "Yeah." He looks back up. "Just make sure the something stays in your fucking pants."

I stare at him, getting his warning loud and clear.

Don't fuck around with Coach's kid. I get it.

But I don't bother refuting his assumption. Because there is something between Leni and me. Something I shouldn't want and yet desire. Something I shouldn't feel but am still leaning into.

It's just dinner. Nothing's happened. I haven't crossed a line.

Yet.

At the look in Avery's eyes, I know he knows it too. "Fuck," he mutters. "Use your head, Miller. Don't throw away everything you've worked for, everything you've earned..."

"I'm not," I say softly, spinning my pint glass in between my palms. "I'm just looking out for her. That's it."

"Yeah." Avery snorts. "I've heard that before."

I'm sure he has. And still, his warning doesn't deter me. Not the way it should.

His conversation doesn't distract me.

I still spend the rest of the night thinking about Leni and our dinner tomorrow night. Even though it's all wrong.

Even though I know better.

9

Leni

I texted Talon a list of ingredients early this morning.

He responded with a green check mark, letting me know he picked up everything we need.

God, I'm nervous. I drag my palms over my denim skirt. I paired it with a sage green bodysuit and plain white sneakers. But riding the elevator up to Talon's place has my heart in my throat and my fingers clutching at the stiff denim.

The only man I've ever cooked for was Craig, and we were living together. It was one of Craig's expectations and I carried out my duties well, fulfilling every whim he had. And it still wasn't enough.

But tonight, I want to cook for Talon. I want to spend time with him, away from any watching eyes.

He's the last man I should date. Not that this is a date or anything.

And still, my heart flutters like butterfly wings against my rib cage, and that trickle of nervous anticipation I used to relish drips down my spine.

Could it be a date? Are we really friends? Or is there potential for more?

When the elevator arrives at his floor, I let out a deep exhale, fix the front pieces of my hair that have fallen out of my loose braid, and hitch my purse that contains a bottle of wine, higher on my shoulder. Then, I stride to Talon's door and knock twice.

He pulls it open a heartbeat later and my eyes widen.

He's dressed casually, in a pair of ripped jeans and a black T-shirt that hugs his biceps, making them pop. His feet are bare, his stance relaxed as he leans against the doorframe, arms crossed over his chest.

"H-hi," I sputter.

A slow smile cuts his gorgeous face. "Sunny Leni." He steps back and gestures me inside. "Welcome."

My gaze darts around his place, noting how clean the space is. The table is set for two, with folded navy napkins and two wine glasses.

"I brought wine," I say, noting the glasses.

Talon grins. "I have some too."

I dip my head in acknowledgement.

"But," he continues. "I can only have a glass or so."

"Preseason." I know all the rules by heart. Dad doesn't put any alcohol consumption limits on his players but he certainly lets them know that he expects them to carry themselves a certain way—with professionalism—and represent the team in a positive light. He always said that by not having too many restrictions, the players generally do things in moderation.

"Yep," Talon agrees, reaching forward to take my shoulder bag from me.

"Oof, this is heavy," he mutters.

"The wine," I admit.

Talon reaches into my bag and removes the bottle, padding toward his kitchen. I follow after him, my eyes darting around his place, looking for clues into his life.

There aren't any.

The walls are white, the furniture simple, and the space tidy. But there's no framed photos or artwork on the wall. No knickknacks on the shelves. Not even a worn paperback on the coffee table.

"Have you lived here long?" I wonder as we enter the kitchen.

"About three years," he admits, surprising me.

Talon places my bag on the kitchen island and turns toward me, his palms open. "Put me to work. I'm ready to learn."

His eagerness to cook with me puts me at ease instantly. Craig hated being in the kitchen. He never cooked anything and I wouldn't be surprised if he didn't know how to boil water.

"All right," I say. "Let's start with the ingredients."

Talon pulls everything out of the refrigerator and lines the ingredients up on the kitchen counter. I wash my hands and survey everything he's purchased for our schnitzel, potatoes, and cucumber salad.

Talon pours us two glasses of wine from the bottle of red he'd already purchased and presses play on a playlist. "Here." He passes me a glass.

I look up, taking in the uncertainty lined in his expression.

He's always so confident. So relaxed and sure of himself. The fact that he's not relaxes me further. We're both navigating the unknown. Together.

I don't know what we're doing; all I know is it feels right.

I feel…better…in his presence.

"Thank you."

He holds his glass up. "To you, Leni. To your new beginning."

I shake my head. "To your season, Talon."

He smirks and we clink glasses and drink.

Then, I explain how we're going to bread and fry the meat and set Talon up chopping cucumbers for the salad. Our conversation flows easily as we prepare dinner, sip our wine, and trade stories.

By the time we sit down to eat, I'm relaxed and relieved.

And Talon is looking at me like I'm the first woman he's ever truly seen. Which makes no damn sense but makes me feel special. Desired.

And it's been so long since I've felt anything close that I don't want this night—this dinner—to end.

I watch Talon as he takes his first bite of the veal schnitzel.

His gray eyes sink to half-mast as he drops his head back and groans.

I lean closer to the table, the edge cutting into my chest. "Do you like it?"

"Leni…" My name is hushed, spoken with reverence. Like crushed seashells mixed with magic.

I shiver from his tone.

He opens his eyes and pierces me with them. "This is the best meal I've ever had in my life."

Nerves skate through me, causing my fingers to curl into the denim of my skirt. I titter out a laugh.

"I'm not kidding," he continues, his voice serious, his expression unreadable. "I've never… No one's ever…" He shakes his head and places his fork down. Folding his hands neatly in front of his plate, he stares at me. "Thank you for dinner."

"You're welcome," I whisper, feeling his appreciation down to my toes.

And having that—Talon's acknowledgement, his gratitude—lights me up like the North Star. Lightness washes through me, sweeping away the shame I've carried for weeks. No, months.

I am enough. I am worthy.

Talon clears his throat and looks away for a beat. When he turns his eyes back on me, they're heavy, ringed with midnight. *Baggage*, my sister Lincoln would say.

But Craig has clear eyes—sky blue—and he inflicted more trauma on me than I could've anticipated.

"No one's ever cooked me dinner before, Len. This…" He pauses to gesture between us. "Is a first for me."

I suck in a breath, his words punching through me. "Never?"

He shakes his head, his lips rolled between his teeth.

"What about your foster parents?" I wonder.

"Foster care wasn't really like that," he admits. "I mean, I ate," he assures me. "But it wasn't a special meal or anything. It was…survival."

"Right," I murmur, sadness rolling through me. For a blink, I can see Talon as a boy. Heather gray-green eyes and a crooked smirk. A backwards baseball cap and a missing front tooth.

And then, the charismatic man at the center of every party, injecting it with laughter. With fun. With surface-level frivolity so no one gets closer or digs deeper.

"I used to cook for my—for Craig—every night," I admit.

A cloud passes through Talon's eyes, but when he blinks, it clears. "He didn't know how damn lucky he was."

The corners of my mouth turn upward but I don't smile. I can't. "I don't think he ever felt that way."

"His loss," Talon replies, his tone harder. Half bite, half bark.

"Maybe," I reply, taking a bite of my dinner.

"Hey." Talon reaches across the table, covering my hand with his. The weight of his palm rests on my fingers, strong and steady. "You deserve the world, Leni. Don't let anyone, especially not some guy in New York, make you feel otherwise."

I dip my head, my fingers desperate to stray to my collarbone. But I keep them pressed against the table, under the warmth of Talon's skin. "I know," I say, even though I don't.

I'm still fighting the thoughts, the memories, the panic of that night. Of several nights.

"Leni?"

I look up and hold Talon's gaze.

"Why did you come home?" There's a thread of hesitation in his voice and I recognize it. I've heard it in Mom's tone, in Marlowe's, and Dad's. Hell, it's the reason why I haven't returned Lincoln's calls since I returned home. She's too close to knowing the truth; I know she suspects it. And for now, I know Mom is buying me time. Eventually, I'll need to connect with my sister and fix the fragility of our relationship. A bond I weakened by being too damn scared.

"It was time," I murmur, hoping the more I say it, the more I'll believe it.

Except the statement doesn't ring completely false. It was time to come home. It was time for...something to give. I just didn't think it would be my relationship.

Talon swipes his thumb over my wrist before removing his hand and nodding, accepting my response for what it is. A white lie.

We resume eating.

I take a big sip of my wine and clear my throat, not wanting anything between us to be awkward. Not when this night has been so effortless.

"How do you feel about the next preseason game?" I ask, knowing Dad has been stressed about the cuts and finalizing the roster.

Talon clears his throat. "We're playing Dallas. It's an away game, but I feel pretty good. The extra time in the pool has helped with flexibility. I'm just trying to stick to my routine and mentally prepare for the season." He looks up and smiles. "For me, mentally being able to tune things out, to have that type of fortitude, is half the battle."

"You need to focus."

"Yeah. No distractions," he says, tilting his head.

Does he mean I'm becoming a distraction?

I can't help but blush at the meaning behind his words.

Is that a good or bad thing?

Talon takes another bite of his dinner and moans again. "Too good, Leni."

"You helped," I remind him.

He laughs. "It never would have come out this well if you weren't running the show."

"Give yourself more credit."

"Nah." He polishes off his wine. "I'd rather give you all the credit. But I'll take the credit for dessert. I got a buttermilk pie—"

"From Annabelle's!" I blurt out, beaming at the thought. Annabelle's pies are the best in Knoxville but they usually sell out within an hour of opening each morning.

"Yes." Talon laughs.

"But you must have gotten there at seven a.m."

Talon shrugs, his eyes catching mine. "It was worth it."

All I hear is *you're worth it.*

And I smile at Talon, feeling my cheeks stretch.

He grins back, easy and familiar.

This is the best non-date dinner I've ever had.

10
TALON

"I got it," I tell Leni as she begins clearing the table.

"We'll do it together," she assures me, stacking our plates. "It will be faster. Plus, you have an early morning tomorrow."

She's not kidding. Tomorrow is an intense practice day as the team prepares for our game against Dallas.

I follow Leni into the kitchen, and we clean up quickly. Then, I grab two plates and forks, carefully balancing the Annabelle's pie box on top, before we head back to the table for dessert.

"I can't believe you're eating pie." She points at me accusingly.

"Don't tell Freddy," I joke back.

Leni grins, leaning against the edge of the table. "Secret's safe with me. I didn't tell Dad I was coming here tonight."

I had wondered about that but didn't want to ask. Hearing her voice it fills me with both relief and disappointment, which is confusing as hell.

Knowing I have Leni's number and took her for tacos is one thing. Inviting her to my home to cook me dinner and share a buttermilk pie from Annabelle's is different and Coach would know it. Hell, Avery already implied as much.

And yet, I hate that she would be embarrassed to tell her Dad she was having dinner with me. There's no man I admire more than Coach Strauss and I wish he could look at me and see more than the Coyotes kicker and a kid with a chip on his shoulder.

"Talon?" Leni asks, gently touching my forearm.

Shit. I shake my head. Force a grin. "Yeah." I grip the back of my neck and shrug. "Probably a good thing, huh?"

She shuffles closer half a step. Her hand lifts to my hip and the second she touches me, my body locks down. But her eyes are wary—hopeful and uncertain—when they meet mine. "Did you want me to tell Dad? Does this… I don't want to make things harder for you. With football," she clarifies.

Somehow, her concern makes it fucking worse. The fact that she cares, the fact that she knows enough about the game, about the team, makes me feel like an ass. And I don't know why.

"No, I know," I murmur.

Leni's fingers curl into the fabric of my shirt and I can't stop myself from wrapping my arm around her waist, placing my palm in the small of her back.

"Leni." What am I going to say? What the hell do I want to say?

Her big eyes plead with me…for what? Her chest heaves, as if she's nervous or…expectant.

Heat sparks between us, shimmering brightly.

"What does this mean, Talon?" She's so damn honest. So fucking vulnerable and it's as endearing as it is terrifying.

"I don't know, Len," I admit truthfully. My other hand lifts in slow motion, cupping her cheek.

She leans into my touch and I feel it everywhere. Her trust is like a live wire to my fucking nervous system. My thumb brushes over her soft skin and I work a swallow. Dragging my thumb down her cheek, I nudge her chin upward, force her to give me her eyes.

And God, they are brilliant. Desire swirls with hope and I stop thinking.

I stop questioning.

I lose my edge, fuck my focus, and drop my mouth to Leni's.

The first brush of my lips with hers is sweeter than any buttermilk pie I've ever tasted. Even Annabelle's.

The tiniest gasp of surprise falls from Leni's mouth and I'm about to pull away when her other hand fists the front of my shirt. She pulls me closer, flush against her body, and I drop one hand to brace it against the table she's pinned against.

Angling my mouth, I deepen our kiss. When Leni's lips part, I slip my tongue inside to meet hers. And it's like fireworks detonate in my head.

Kissing Leni is all color and spark. Promise and purpose.

I take my time, feeling the smoothness of her curves, letting my mouth linger over hers, lengthening our connection and our kiss until we're both breathless.

When Leni pulls back, she giggles nervously and even that sound—sweet, so fucking sweet—sends a rush through my bloodstream.

Her chest heaves and I have to avert my gaze before I pull her shirt clear over her head.

"Leni." I drop my forehead to hers. With each breath, reality seeps back in and the realization of what I just did—of what I just took—glares back at me.

I kissed my coach's daughter.

Fuck.

"Leni," I repeat, with more urgency this time.

She looks up sharply at what she hears in my tone.

Already, the hope in her eyes is stamped out with understanding and I feel like an asshole for what I'm about to say.

"I shouldn't have kissed you," I whisper. Fuck, but I wanted to.

She rears back like I pushed her and I shuffle back several steps, adding distance. I grip the back of my neck again, this time squeezing tight enough to press some fucking common sense in.

Leni wipes her fingers against her swollen lips, as if wiping away my kiss, and I wince.

She's so beautiful. So fucking lovely.

There's that word again.

"Len—"

"Why not?" she asks, a challenge brightening her eyes.

"Because," I say, almost pleading with her.

You're out of my league.

I don't know how to do this.

I've never had a real relationship.

Your father is like a father figure to me.

"Because of football," she whispers, understanding dawning in her expression. "No distractions, right?" This time, her tone is harder.

And I swear. Partly because it's the truth and partly because I didn't even fucking think about it. About football and the team.

When I kissed Leni, all I thought about was her and how I'd never be enough. Never measure up.

And then, I thought about disappointing Coach. Not as my coach but as a man.

Not that Leni would understand. If I told her that, she'd think I'm feeding her bullshit lines.

I clear my throat. "Right." I force the word out. Watch it pierce the air.

Witness Leni's expression fall.

Welcome the kick that lands in my gut.

"I'm sorry, Talon," Leni says, hurt evident in her tone. Her eyebrows furrow and confusion crosses her face. "I don't know why I..." She trails off and I desperately wish she would complete her sentence. Finish her thought. She doesn't. Instead, she squares her shoulders and looks at me again. "I'm sorry."

I don't want her apology. This wasn't her fault—it was me crossing a line and taking something I don't deserve but desire anyway.

"I'm not," I say.

She frowns.

Fuck. I'm sending her mixed messages.

"You have nothing to be sorry about," I amend.

She dips her head and reaches for her shoulder bag. "I should get going."

"Wait." I toss an arm out and she recoils, flinching. But I'm reaching for the pie box and when she notes that, relief filters over her expression.

What the hell? Did she think I was going to...what?

"Take this." I press the pie box into her hands.

"No, I—I can't."

"Please." I leave it in her grasp. Force myself not to brush a lock of her hair behind her ear. "Tonight, this dinner, it meant a lot to me, Leni."

"Yeah," she says. "Me too." But her tone is clipped and I know she's just as confused, maybe even a little embarrassed, as I am.

I hate that I made her feel that way. I hate that I messed shit up between us.

But most of all, I hate that when I walk her to the door and say good night, I do nothing to erase the look of dejectedness off her face.

Leaning back in the airplane seat, I close my eyes. I'm fucking exhausted. Partly from practice and partly from the shit sleep I've gotten the past few nights.

"What gives?" Callaway asks, dropping into the seat beside me.

I open an eye and glare at him. "Can't you sit somewhere else?"

"Nope," Crawford offers cheerily, sitting across the aisle from Avery.

I groan. "I'm going to sleep on this flight."

"Don't let me keep you awake then," Callaway says, crossing an ankle over his knee and jabbing it into my quad.

"What the hell?" I mutter, pushing his knee away.

Crawford snickers on Avery's other side.

"What's going on with you?" Callaway hisses. "Please don't tell me you slept—"

"What?" I interrupt, stopping his trail of thought before he can voice it aloud. On a plane with the team and Coach. "Of course not."

His eyes narrow. "You don't know who I was about to say."

I wince.

"Miller, this isn't a fucking joke," Callaway mutters.

"Keep your voice down." I jerk my head to the side, knowing that Crawford is trying to eavesdrop. Luckily, his phone buzzes and since we're still on the tarmac—and it's Nova—he picks up.

Half a second later, he's making fucking baby talk and I breathe a little easier knowing that nothing will distract Crawford from his baby girl. Not even scandalous gossip.

"What happened?" Avery presses.

"I kissed her," I admit, not even caring that I'm confiding in him. Because I have no one else to confide in.

I don't have a Marlowe or a Lincoln. I only have my team.

And as much as Callaway is Coach's golden boy, he knows a thing or two about scandal.

Avery drops his head back and sighs. "You can get in any woman's pants, why—"

"I don't know," I cut him off.

What I don't say is that it's not just about getting in Leni's pants. It's more than that. I just don't understand what the more is.

Why do I care so much? Why am I interested in her day? Or the debutante ball?

Or react to vibes from that dumbass, Toby?

Avery scrubs a hand down his face. "Listen, I'm not a fucking saint. What I put Mila through was messed up and even now…" Avery trails off, but I know what he's implying.

He's been with a lot of women and hasn't thought twice about it.

"But when it affects the team…I learned my lesson. I've tried to steer clear of any scandal or anything that could disrupt dynamics. The season hasn't even officially started, Talon. Coach's daughter? Come on, man. Think about what you're doing."

I sigh and tap my head against the headrest.

"We're taking off in three," Crawford says.

Beside me, Avery swears softly and shoves on his headphones.

I do the same and close my eyes, feigning sleep.

But I don't get a wink of shut-eye the entire flight to Dallas. Instead, I think about Leni. And that fucking kiss.

The soft curve of her cheek. The smooth strands of her hair. The heat of her body pressed against mine. Her sweet, full lips…

By the time we land, I'm in a shitty mood. Callaway gives me space and the rest of the team steers clear.

When I check into the hotel, I fire off a lame, generic message to Leni.

> Me: Need me to grab anything for this weekend?

And I'm not surprised that when I wake in the morning, she keeps me on read.

11

Leni

Marylee clears her throat beside me, and I flinch.

"Pardon?" I ask, my cheeks flushing. I spaced out and didn't catch a word Sarah said.

Sarah leans forward. "The main flower in the centerpieces. Roses or peonies?"

"Oh." I sit up straighter, shaking my head to clear it. "Peonies." I tilt my head, mentally running through the color palette. "Cream and peach."

"Great," Marylee agrees, making a note in her binder.

The conversation resumes—canapés selection and the signature cocktail—and my thoughts wander again.

The way I clung to the material of Talon's shirt.

The warmth of his hand on my cheek, the brush of his thumb over my lips.

His lips—full and parted—arcing over mine.

Stormy gray eyes, brimming with emotions.

A kiss I lost myself in. A man who makes me feel too many things I yearn for.

I shouldn't have kissed you.

The words I knew all along, but it took Talon saying them for me to remember.

He's off-limits.

And I'm a terrible judge of where to draw the line.

The months I stayed with Craig. The apologies I accepted when I should have packed my bags.

My fingers skate over my collarbone—a memory that won't fade even though the bruises did—and other thoughts infiltrate.

The scent of scotch.

Craig's wild eyes, edged with anger. The twist of his mouth and tightness of his grip.

The condescending words that fell from his lips.

And the messages. A whole thread of unanswered texts.

> Craig: Leni, are you ready to talk yet?

> Craig: You can't avoid me forever, sweetheart. I know we argued but moving out was a mistake. Breaking up was a mistake.

> Craig: I need you, baby. Give me the chance to fight for us. Call me.

> Craig: Leni, come on now.

> Lincoln: Leni, stop avoiding me! I miss you! Call me, please.

> Craig: What game are you playing? Do you think you can win?

> Craig: You know I'll come for you, right? I won't let you leave me, Leni. Not forever.

> Craig: You belong to me, baby. You're mine. And you better not fucking forget it.

> Talon: Need me to grab anything for this weekend?

Argh! It seems like my MO is indecision. I can't respond. Can't react.

Can't focus on the conversation unfolding around me.

A headache forms, pinching at my temples and gathering over my eyebrows.

My knee bounces beneath the table and my heart rate thrums in my eardrums.

Failure. Not enough. What the hell am I doing with my life?

I glance around the group of women I admire and wonder what they would say if they knew.

Knew that I stayed with a man who put his hands on me.

Knew that I was lusting for one of my dad's players.

Knew how fucking scared and confused I feel most moments of most days.

I'm not a role model for young women. I'm not a woman who has her shit together—despite the credibility I've gained by living in New York City. I'm not marriage material. Or girl boss vibes.

I'm floundering. Making one mistake after another and harboring so many damn regrets, I'm drowning in them.

Faltering spectacularly. Incapable of answering a damn text message. Of putting Craig in his place. Unable to press charges the way I know I should.

I shouldn't have kissed you.

I'm a fraud. A fake. A fucking joke.

And I can't take it anymore.

Jumping up from my chair, I gather my belongings.

"Leni?" Sarah asks.

"I'm so sorry," I stutter, my hand wrapping around the base of my throat.

Nausea churns in my stomach.

"I suddenly don't feel well," I admit, relieved I don't have to add "liar" to my list of faults. Right now, I feel terrible.

Like I'm coming apart at the seams.

"Oh, no. Take care of yourself." Marylee's eyebrows pinch together. At the concern in her gaze, I know I must look ill. "John?" she calls out to a member of the club's staff. "Can you retrieve Ms. Strauss's car?"

"Absolutely, ma'am." John scrambles toward the exit.

Anna Louise packs up my binder. She passes it to me with an understanding, compassionate squeeze to my forearm.

And their understanding—their care—makes me feel worse. I don't deserve them. I don't deserve this position on the organizing committee when I'm sure there was a list of more qualified candidates.

I don't deserve anything.

Certainly not Talon.

I shouldn't have kissed you.

I mutter my thanks and wave away the extra sets of supportive hands as I make my way to the main entrance. I'm so relieved to see my car, I almost hug John.

I dump my belongings in the passenger seat, slide behind the wheel, and point my car toward home.

But I only make it two streets before I pull to the shoulder of the road. Sobs wrack through my body and the dam finally breaks.

I crack and I cry.

My chest heaves and my shoulders shake. Dropping my forehead to the steering wheel, I clutch it with both hands. Everything I've held on to for months comes pouring out of me in a deluge of tears, snotty sighs, and then, hysterical hiccups.

Anger and pain.

Betrayal and hurt.

Frustration and confusion.

Uncertainty over the future.

And so much fucking shame.

It pours out, tracks down my cheeks, drops onto my bare thighs.

It's ugly and messy. Honest and heartbreaking.

I don't know how long I cry. Only that my cell phone lights up several times in the cupholder it sits in. I can't bear to read any more messages I'll most likely ignore so I don't bother checking.

Instead, I sit on the side of the road until I'm calm enough to lift my head. The blood rushes there, leaving me dizzy. I wipe my fingers over my cheeks and take a deep, cleansing breath.

God, what the hell is wrong with me?

Flipping down the sun visor, I wince at my reflection. I really do look ill. I snap it shut and lean back, pressing my head into the headrest as my breathing regulates.

And the exhaustion hits.

By the time I park in my parents' driveway, I'm drained. I grip my purse and phone but don't have the bandwidth to read the messages on screen. Instead, I make it to my room, drop my purse, strip out of my clothes and tug on comfy pajamas, and collapse on my bed.

Pulling the covers over my shoulders, I drift into a weightless sleep that clears my mind, numbs my emotions, and allows my muscles to unclench and my body to relax.

I sleep hard.

"Wake up, sleepyhead," Marlowe says, shaking my shoulder gently.

I stir, blinking slowly as her expression comes into view. "Mar?"

"Hey," my best friend says, leaning against the pillows propped up along my headboard. "You were out cold."

"Yeah," I agree, stretching silently. Marlowe's had a key to Mom and Dad's house since the fourth grade. It's not uncommon for her to pop by unannounced, but it's been a long time since she's done so since I've been away for two years. "What's going on?" I frown, noting the uncertainty in her expression.

Marlowe sighs and shakes her head as I pull myself into a seated position.

"Marlowe?" I press. *Did something else happen with Grandpa McIntyre?*

My best friend sighs. "Something's going on with my family."

I inch closer to her, laying my head on her shoulder. "I heard about your grandfather."

She shakes her head. "It's more than that, Leni. Adi is so stressed about the debutante ball; my grandfather is awful. Poor Samantha. But my parents…"

"What?" I whisper, nervous. Marlowe's parents aren't as involved in her life the way my parents are in mine, but they're present.

"I don't know," she admits. "Something is going on. They've both been acting differently…around me, around each other. Whenever I ask, they say it's just the stress of dealing with Grandpa, but I think it's something else."

"Oh, Marlowe. Why didn't you tell me?" I ask, wincing as soon as the words are out of my mouth.

Marlowe shifts and looks at me. "Don't take this the wrong way, Len, but you haven't really been around lately. And I don't mean physically. When you first moved to New York, we still talked all the time but after you moved in with Craig…"

"Things changed," I fill in the blank. Of course, she's right. The more controlling Craig became, the more I tried to mold myself to be the woman he wanted, the more I pulled away from my family and friends. The more distance I put between myself and Marlowe. "But you have Toby," I add, trying to diffuse my guilt.

"It's not the same thing," Marlowe says, her green eyes glinting. "And you know it."

I sigh and nod. "I'm sorry."

"I am too. Besides, things with Toby are…"

I wait for her to continue. When she doesn't, I press my shoulder lightly against hers.

"Rocky," she finally says. "Whenever we're together, we drink. Usually, I drink too much and…things are different with him too."

"For how long?" I wonder.

She snorts. "I don't know. We've always been complicated."

"Yeah," I agree, thinking of Craig. Were we complicated from the beginning, and it took me too long to realize it? There were red flags that I ignored, mentally coloring them beige instead.

"What the hell happened with Craig anyway?" Marlowe asks, reading my mind. This time, there's a glint to her eyes, an understanding, that wasn't there the first time she asked me when I arrived home.

I close my eyes and snuggle against her shoulder. "It was bad, Mar," I murmur, my voice scratchy.

"How bad?" She squeezes my hand, a silent show of strength. And one I need if I'm going to admit all the things I've been bottling up for months.

"I had to leave." My fingers twist together, my nails cutting into my hands. "Craig was…complicated. Controlling." I hold my breath the second the words pierce the air.

Marlowe wraps an arm around my shoulders, and I snuggle closer. She doesn't say anything and her acceptance, her lack of judgement, encourages me to continue speaking.

"When things became stressful at work, he would drink. And when he would drink, he'd get mean. Violent."

Her hand tightens on my shoulder, her fingers digging into the fabric of my shirt. "Did he ever hit you?"

I nod, my eyes welling with tears. "It was only—"

"Don't do that," she cuts me off. "Even one time isn't a justification, Leni."

I close my eyes as a tear slides down my cheek. "I know."

"But you left. You came home," Marlowe points out.

"I should have left sooner." I sound miserable. But how could I not? Admitting this, even to my best friend, is like shining a glaring spotlight on all my mistakes. On all the times I should have spoken up but didn't. Should have left but stayed.

"You got out, Leni. Don't look back and beat yourself up. The truth is you're here and you're safe. You're back."

I pull in a deep breath, hold it in my chest for several heartbeats, and release it. "I'm back."

"Have you talked to anyone? Like, a professional? Or the police?"

"No," I admit, feeling defeated.

"You still can." Her voice is gentle.

"Yeah," I say. "I'll think about it." But will I?

"You seem more like yourself than you have in over a year," Marlowe comments. "Calmer. Happier. Just...more you."

I nod, smiling softly. "I feel more like myself too."

Except for Craig's messages, which continue to light up my phone, I feel stronger too. More in control of my future. More capable of making life decisions.

While a small part of me wonders, and worries, if Craig will show up in Knoxville, a larger part of me knows I'm safe. Dad and his entire football team would have my back and knowing that some of the strongest, fastest, and biggest men in the country would show up for me eases my mind. It's something Craig knows too and I imagine that's why he's still sending me texts instead of knocking on Dad's front door.

"Does Talon Miller have anything to do with that?" Marlowe wonders and I hear the curiosity laced in her tone.

I'm silent for a long beat before a tiny chuckle falls from my lips.

"Oh my God!" Marlowe swats at me. "Are y'all dating?"

"No, no." I shake my head. "Nothing like that."

"But you want to?" she presses.

"We kissed!" I squeal. Then, I smack a hand over my mouth. Fresh tears well in my eyes and Marlowe's gaze studies my face. "Marlowe, what is wrong with me? I just got out of a terrible, dangerous relationship. And I'm giddy because one of my dad's football players has been tasked with chaperoning me next weekend."

Marlowe grins slowly. "There's nothing wrong with you, Leni. You just forgot what butterflies feels like. It's no surprise that Craig stopped making you feel anything but fucking nervous. He strikes me as a dude with a small dick who needs to overcompensate by being fucking evil."

I roll my lips together before another laugh erupts. "He did have a small, limp dick!"

Marlowe's eyes widen at my outburst and then, the tension, the past year of space, the heartache and hurts, shift. Crack. Implode. Erupt.

And we both start howling.

Sobbing.

Reaching for each other, hugging and holding on, like our lives depend on it.

The soft cotton of Marlowe's thin T-shirt absorbs my tears. Her long nails tangle in the ends of my hair. And our laughter, bordering on hysterical, mingles in the space between us. Around us.

Everything is a fucking disaster.

Marlowe's family is falling apart.

My romantic life is in fucking shambles as I lust after one of my dad's players even though my abusive ex-boyfriend is blowing up my phone.

But one of the missing pieces of my life snaps back in place, moving the puzzle closer to completion.

I have my best friend back. Really, truly back. Without the awkward silences. Without being confused about how much I can confide. Without wondering if she'll judge me for being weak, pathetic, naïve.

"We're back, Leni," Marlowe confirms my thoughts, and I hug her harder.

"I'm sorry I allowed so much time and space to pass."

"Don't do that either," she reminds me.

I snort, she laughs, and then, we cry.

It's cathartic and necessary. It's a homecoming I never knew I needed but cling to with both hands.

I have my best friend back and knowing that fills me with lightness.

With courage.

With hope.

My growling stomach interrupts our reunion.

"You need to fucking eat," Marlowe admonishes. "You're too damn thin."

"It's the nerves," I share, not holding anything back anymore.

Marlowe's brow furrows. "But you're home now."

"He's still texting me." I unlock my phone screen and shove it into her hands.

"Leni!" Marlowe shrieks, waving around my phone. "This is serious."

I wrinkle my nose. "Do you think? He could just be—"

"No. Craig is fucking unstable. He put his hands on you."

"Shh!" I interject, slamming my palm over her mouth. The last thing I need is for one of my parents to overhear that truth.

Marlowe rolls her eyes, and I remove my hand.

"Your dad is still at work and your mom went to Pilates. I saw her on my way inside," Marlowe explains. "But you should tell them, Leni. This isn't something to take lightly." She passes me back my phone. "I don't trust him and neither should you. My parents made that mistake and if Samantha wasn't the woman she is, my grandfather could have very easily ended up hurting Adi."

I suck in a sharp breath, recognizing the truth in her voice. It could have been Adeline—a point I wasn't willing to consider until Marlowe said it.

"I'm sorry, Marlowe."

She sighs and drags the back of her hand over her eyes. "So am I."

"Want some pie from Annabelle's?" I offer, remembering Talon's parting gift.

I shouldn't have kissed you.

Hurtful words but at least he gave me the pie to eat my feelings.

Marlowe quirks an eyebrow. "What kind?"

"Buttermilk."

She grins. "Why the hell are we still sitting here, crying, when we can be inhaling pie and divulging every detail about your kiss with Talon?"

"Shh!"

Marlowe laughs and slips off my bed. "I want to hear everything."

"It's not that exciting. He said he shouldn't have kissed me afterwards." I flick a hand dismissively even though I hardly feel indifferent about it.

"Well, of course, he did. He could fuck his entire career and he knows it. But clearly, knowing he shouldn't kiss you and being able to keep his lips off yours are two different things." Marlowe fans herself and shoots me a smile.

I gape at her. In a handful of sentences, she's managed to reframe the entire scenario that led me to go to bed early. "Do you really think so?"

"Totally." By the sincerity in her tone and the flicker in her eyes, I know she's being truthful. She really believes that Talon wanted to kiss me.

Another sliver of hope flickers to life in my heart and while I know I should shut it down, I don't.

It feels too good. Right.

Hm. Is that how Talon felt too?

"I want all the details with my pie," Marlowe reminds me.

"Right." I slide off my bed and jam my feet into fluffy slippers. "Are you excited for your birthday weekend?"

"I am now that you and Talon are coming."

I glance at her over my shoulder as we descend the stairs toward the kitchen. "Toby?" I ask the obvious.

She shrugs. "Things have been weird lately. Just…different. I don't know, Len. I have this feeling that everything is about to change. And even though I can't pinpoint what or how, it's unshakeable."

I flip on the kettle for our tea and stack two plates on top of the pie box. "Would that be the worst thing?"

She looks at me, her expression curious. Not upset or scared. Just unsure. "I don't know."

"Well, you know you can talk to me about anything," I remind her as I slice two pieces of pie.

"And you too," she says seriously. "I can't do this again." She gestures between us before sitting down at the kitchen table and reaching for her plate. "I need you too much, Len. You're my best friend."

I pass her a fork. "Marlowe, you're like my other sister. I'm sorry."

"Speaking of sisters, you need to reach out to Lincoln."

"She called you?"

"Twice," Marlowe confirms.

I sigh. "I miss her too."

"She'll understand, Leni. She loves you. We both do."

"I love you, too."

Marlowe smirks and lifts her fork in the air. I tap it with mine. "We're back, baby."

12
TALON

I reread her text and grin. Damn, Sunny Leni kept me on fucking read the past few days and now, she's letting me know that I can come pick her up for our drive out to the lake.

A ride which promises to be awkward since I fucking kissed her and then, nothing. She left, I went to Dallas, and we haven't spoken about it. About anything.

She hasn't even showed up to the pool the last few nights. She's avoiding me and I'm going into this weekend with her blind.

Fuck. I messed this up.

"You good?" Avery asks as I toss a pair of sneakers in my bag.

"Yep." I grin cockily, like I'm not mentally floundering. "All straight."

"Really? You feel good about this weekend with Leni? Y'all talked?"

"Not yet, but I'm sure it'll be fine. A few days have passed. It's all good now, right?" I say, hoping he confirms my assessment of the situation.

West Crawford chuckles. I glance at where he's straddling a bench. "A few days passed with no contact? Bro, you're fucked. Shit's going to be awkward and intense until you clear the air so if I was you, I'd do that straight away. Especially if you want to enjoy your days off."

"Damn," I mutter, fearing that he's right.

"Leni's reasonable," Avery offers, lowering his voice. While I imagine West knows exactly what we're talking about, he never asked for confirmation or details. He's a good guy like that—isn't one for gossip or talking shit.

"I hurt her feelings," I mutter.

Avery sighs. "Listen, just clear the air like West said. Show up for her, keep an eye on her, and try to have a good fucking weekend. But make sure she has fun, Miller. The last thing you want is for Coach to ride your ass the entire season because you screwed over his little girl."

I close my eyes and nod. I know Avery is right. Hell, the majority of my football team is comprised of playboys who can't keep it in their pants. And yet, all of them know more about relationships and how to navigate them than I do.

"All right." I stand and shoulder my bag. "I'll see you guys on Monday."

"Take it easy, Talon," West offers, shooting me an encouraging grin.

Avery smacks my back in farewell. Gage and Cohen flip their chins in my direction, the two of them lost in conversation.

I lift a hand and exit the locker room. I'm nearly to the parking lot when Coach's voice booms out.

"Miller! Just the man I was looking for." Coach hurries toward me.

"Hey, Coach. How's it going?" I ask.

"Good, good." He clasps my shoulder. "You all set for this weekend?"

"Yep. Leni said to swing by to pick her up at six."

"Good. She's been…different, these past few days."

"Has she?" I mutter, wondering where Coach is going with this.

His fingers flex involuntarily on my shoulder, and I clear my throat.

Did Leni tell him I kissed her? Did she say anything about the night we had dinner? Is something else going on that I don't know about?

And why the fuck do I hate it so much? I've always felt comfortable around Coach. I could always count on him to have my back.

But, clearly, not when it comes to his own daughter. His flesh and blood.

I'm out of my element and I don't know what the hell to do about it.

"Keep an eye on her, Miller. I'm trusting you," Coach warns, his words slamming into me like a punch to the gut.

"I got it, Coach. Don't worry."

He snorts, as if he can't not worry.

Damn.

"Call me if you need anything. And try to enjoy the weekend."

"Will do," I say as he gives me one last, hard squeeze and ambles down the hallway.

I push out an exhale and grip the back of my neck. My thoughts whirl as my stomach tightens. I have no clue what I'm getting into this weekend.

All I know is I'm hung up on Leni Strauss.

Her father would fucking kill me.

To an extent, he can determine the trajectory of my career.

I'd never want to put the guys on my team in a compromising position. But I also can't get the memory of Leni, the feel of my mouth on hers, out of my mind. I've thought about her since the moment she walked out of my condo, an Annabelle's pie box tucked under her arm.

I've gone out of my mind that she kept me on read the past few days, not bothering to reply to my text message.

Up until twenty minutes ago, I wasn't one-hundred percent sure if I was still going to the lake house this weekend. Like a fool, I hoped I was, and I packed a bag accordingly, tossing it into the back of my SUV before coming to the training facility for a morning workout.

Now, I'm ready to go, with energy buzzing in my limbs and concern spooling in my mind.

The last thing I want to do is go home and kill time, waiting for six p.m.

Fuck that.

Pulling out my phone, I tap out a message.

> Me: I'm done early. I'll be by in twenty.

Three bubbles dance across the bottom of our text thread. Stop. Begin again. Stop.

> Leni: Now???

> Me: Now. We need to talk, Leni.

> Leni: You can't just demand that we need to talk, Talon.

> Me: Fine. Can I take you for an early dinner, please? I'd like to talk to you.

> Me: I'm a dumbass and I messed up.

> Me: I want to have a fun weekend with you.

> Me: And I want to apologize—for real— before we begin our drive.

There. I laid it all out. I know I messed up. I shouldn't have kissed her, but I did anyway. I crossed the fucking line and now, I need to backtrack. But ignoring her or pushing her away isn't going to help when we're going to spend the next two days together.

The dots appear again.

Leni: Fine. Thirty minutes.

I grin.

Me: See you soon, babe.

Leni: 😕

Chuckling softly to myself, I slip my phone into my pocket and stride out of the training facility.

The sky is clear, a bright blue without a cloud in sight. The heat wraps around me and I soak it in. After a handful of years in cool, rainy Oregon, I've come to love the hot days of Tennessee. My flip-flops smack against the pavement as I walk to my SUV.

I drop my gym bag in the trunk, beside my weekend bag, and grin.

I'm going to have a good fucking weekend with Leni. I'm not going to cross any lines or put either of us in a compromising position.

We're friends, right?

Friends can hang out, chill, and have a good time together.

That's what this weekend will be for me and Leni.

I can feel it.

I was fucking wrong.

Shocking, right?

But what the hell was I thinking?

Parked in front of Leni's parents' house, I watch as she glides down the front porch. She was already outside and waiting when I pulled up and, Christ, does she look gorgeous.

Her hair bounces around her shoulders, her eyes—that gorgeous cerulean blue—are hidden behind a pair of over-sized sunglasses, but I can imagine them sparking.

And how messed up is that? I can imagine what her eyes look like as she watches me pull into her driveway.

I put the gearstick in park before sliding out.

"Hey!" I lift a hand in greeting.

"Hey," she calls back, her expression carefully neutral. What the hell does that mean?

I move toward her, taking her cute, pink weekender bag off her shoulder.

"I got it," she mutters while letting me slip it off her arm.

I fight my eye roll and move to the trunk, stowing her bag with mine.

"You ready?" I ask.

"Yep," she says, widening her stance as if we're about to face off.

Hell, are we?

I fight my grin.

Leni slides into my passenger seat and I slip back behind the steering wheel. We pull out of her driveway in silence, and I point my ride toward a decent burger joint Gage introduced me to.

The tension pulls between us, taut and ready to snap, like a rubber band.

At the first red light, I decide to be the bigger person.

"I'm sorry—" I start.

"I wanted to kiss you," she admits at the same time.

"What?" I stare at her.

Leni sighs and pushes her head back into the headrest.

Her fingers twist in her lap. Before I can stop myself, I reach over to clasp both of her hands in one of mine.

"Why are you sorry?" she asks.

Shit. The light turns green, and I ease the SUV forward.

"I don't want to make you uncomfortable. And I don't want to cross any lines."

"Because of my dad."

"Football is my entire life," I admit, half apology, half stating a fact.

"Yeah, I get that."

"No." I shake my head, sliding my palm over the top of the steering wheel. "It's really like the only thing I have going for me. I'm not like you, Len. I didn't grow up with parents and options and security." I blow out a breath.

She turns toward me and pushes those sunglasses up onto the top of her head. Her blue eyes hold mine and fuck if I don't want to drown in them.

"I'm not saying this to upset you. I'm saying it so you understand where I'm coming from. I don't know how to do this." I squeeze her fingers. "I don't know how to do anything, cultivate any type of relationship, that isn't connected to my team. It's all I've ever known."

"You've never…dated?" she asks, confusion in her tone.

"Not for real. I've taken women out on dates, yes. Wined and dined them? Sure. Saw a few more than two or three times." I squint, trying to recall the women I had brief flings with. "Twice," I confirm. "But a real relationship? With talks about the future and going to meet a woman's parents and being included in conversations about their lives or careers?" I shake my head. "Never."

Her mouth drops open, and I note the shock in her irises.

"Kissing you, hell, being with you, it's confusing for me. I like hanging with you, Leni. I like talking and saying shit that's real and substantial for once. But…" I sigh and pause as I pull into the parking lot of the burger place. "But you're my coach's daughter. Your dad pulled me through a really dark time and showed up for me when my mom passed."

Leni sucks in a deep breath, horrified. I squeeze her fingers again.

Parking the SUV, I turn it off and look at Leni.

"I don't want to disappoint a man I admire so much, Leni."

"Why would you disappoint him?" she wonders.

I snort. She's so naïve. Sweet and good and big-hearted. "Babe, I'm not good enough for you."

"Talon."

"I'm not saying that to upset you either. Just stating a fact. I'm not in your league. I know it. Your dad knows it. And deep down, I hope you know it too." I clear my throat, feeling out of sorts. I never put myself out there like this but if we're going to get through the weekend—and remain friends, are we friends?—I need to be honest.

"The fact that you would say all that makes you worthy of any woman you want to be with," Leni replies, her voice soft, her eyes sad. "I've sworn off football players my entire life, Talon. You're the first one I've ever kissed. And I wanted to."

"Len," I breathe out. "There are things at stake, our futures to consider." Fuck. How am I already waffling? For all my tough talk, I know I'll crumble to whatever Leni wants.

The fact that you would say all that makes you worthy of any woman you want to be with.

She sees me, a version of me, that no one's ever taken the time to notice before. And fuck if that's not heady. Healing.

"I know," she sighs. "I just wanted you to know that I wanted that kiss with you."

I smirk, releasing her hands to cup her cheek. "Me too, babe. More than you can understand. I want to have fun with you this weekend. I don't want to do this awkward shit. I don't know how. If you've got something to say to me, say it.

If I do something you don't like, tell me. If you want something from me, ask."

Her eyes widen as she searches my expression. "That simple, huh?"

"That simple, Len. I'm a guy who's never been in any type of real relationship before. I don't have the skill set to navigate a woman's feelings without her clueing me in."

Leni huffs out a laugh. "All right. I'll be straightforward."

I brush my thumb over her high cheekbone before dropping my hand. "I appreciate that." I stare at her for a long beat, noting the sparkle in her eyes, the curve of her bottom lip, the light dance of freckles across the bridge of her nose. "Want to eat a burger?"

She chuckles and rolls her eyes. "Sure. We'll probably hit some traffic so it's best to eat now."

We exit my SUV. As we step forward, I place my hand on the small of her back and instead of inching forward, she presses back into my touch. It feels natural. Right.

But I don't read too much into that. I can't.

"Happy birthday, beautiful!" I hug Marlowe hard, kissing her temple.

"I'm so happy you're here, Len," she breathes back, wrapping an arm around my waist.

While Marlowe certainly knows how to party, there's an edge to her that I don't understand. She's not tipsy and she's not at ease the way I expected her to be. Instead, she almost looks relieved that Talon and I are here.

"What's going on?" I lower my voice.

Marlowe shakes her head, emotion swelling in her eyes. "Toby's drunk."

What else is new? Toby can't handle his liquor for shit. "And?"

"He's saying things…things that don't make sense," Marlowe admits. "I don't understand."

"Like what?" I ask, a warning bell clanging in my head. Is he angry? Is he spewing the type of shit that precedes a smack to the cheek? Or a bottle of scotch thrown across a room in a moment of anger?

"Stuff about my family, my parents." She sucks in a breath, her eyes darting around. While the deck of Toby's parents' lake house contains clusters of people—some of Marlowe's and my friends from high school, most of Toby's friends from God knows where—no one is paying attention to us.

"Happy birthday, Marlowe," Talon says, leaning around me to grin at my best friend. "I'll go grab some beers."

"That'd be great. Thanks." I smile at Talon, relieved that he gets it. For a guy who has never had a girlfriend before, he doesn't suck at reading social clues.

Not that I'm his girlfriend or anything.

"What stuff? Grandpa McIntyre?"

Marlowe shakes her head. She blinks rapidly, as if to hold back tears. "He's saying my dad isn't my dad."

"What?" I gasp. "Why would he say that? And how the hell would he—" The words die in my throat because Marlowe's dad and Toby's dad have been best buddies for ages. Since they were in high school.

"I don't know. I don't understand. But the way he's saying it, Len, and the way my parents have been acting lately... A part of me thinks Toby is telling the truth. That he knows more about my family than I do."

"Where is he?" I ask, glancing around the deck. Toby isn't on it. Figures; he's such a shitty boyfriend.

Marlowe shrugs. "He took the boat out with a few of the guys."

"Oh," I say, not commenting more.

Marlowe offers a watery smile. "I know what you're thinking."

I sigh. We promised we'd be straight with each other. "You deserve better."

"Do I?" The fact that she asks is alarming. What happened to my fun-loving, larger-than-life, confident friend?

In two years, I know I changed. I had to. But standing here, studying Marlowe, I realize she has too. Toby, her family, and the circumstances of the past few years have tarnished her shine.

"Yes," I say, my voice clear.

Marlowe snorts. I wrap an arm around her waist and she drops her head to my shoulder. "I'm so happy you're here, Leni."

I kiss the top of her head, realizing how much we need each other. Now more than ever. "I am too, Len. And this is going to be a great birthday."

She laughs and shakes her head, knowing I'm full of shit.

"It can be," I continue. "This year should be the year you go after what you want. If that's answers, get them. You deserve better, across the board. Don't settle for less."

Marlowe holds my gaze for a long moment before nodding. "You're right."

"I know I am."

"And you need to take your own advice too."

I roll my eyes. "Calling me on my bullshit, huh?"

"Someone has to." Marlowe grins and holds out her hand.

I shake it. "To the next year."

"Another trip around the sun," she says.

"And a fresh beer," Talon says, stepping up with three Solo cups balanced between his hands.

"Thanks, Talon," Marlowe says, helping herself to a beer.

"Can't be empty-handed on your birthday." He winks at her.

We toast to Marlowe's birthday. I take a pull of my beer and smack my lips together. "Yuengling?"

Marlowe nods.

"Damn, Leni," Talon remarks. "Didn't take you for a beer girl."

Marlowe chortles. "She's German."

"Fair," Talon remarks.

"I'm partial to pilsners, particularly Beck's," I share.

Talon smirks. "I'll make a note of that." He wraps an arm around my waist and I lean closer, as if pulled by a magnet.

"Y'all are cute together," Marlowe comments.

I straighten from her words, tension trickling through my body.

Is anyone taking photos tonight? Will Dad see them and wonder why Talon and I seem so comfortable around each other? Is Talon—

"Thanks," he says easily, taking another pull of his beer. He isn't bothered by Marlowe's observation. In fact, his hand splays wider on my lower back, his pinky slipping slightly underneath the band of my jeans.

Marlowe gives me a look and I roll my lips together to keep from cheesing too damn hard.

I have no idea what Talon and I are doing. It's a delicate dance. A little push, a little pull. But it's exciting and exhilarating. It's a breath of fresh air after the shit Craig put me through. And I want to enjoy it.

The sound of a boat engine pulls our attention, and we all turn toward the dock as Toby drives up. The guys on the boat are rowdy, much drunker than the rest of us hanging on the deck, and a sheen of panic slips across Marlowe's expression.

"I'll be right back," she says, stepping toward the dock.

"Let us know if you need backup," Talon offers, correctly reading the situation.

Not for the first time, I'm relieved, hell, maybe even a little grateful, that Dad insisted he come along this weekend.

Talon's arm tightens around me and I shuffle closer, resting my head against his strong chest.

"She can do better than him," he echoes my thoughts.

"Much better," I agree before glancing up at him. "Thank you for coming with me, Talon. I know this isn't how you'd want to spend a day off but—"

"I'm right where I want to be, Leni," he says sweetly. Seriously. One side of his mouth tugs upward and he leans down to drop a kiss to the crown of my head.

We stand like that for a while, watching the guys get off the boat. Noting the argument that erupts between Marlowe and Toby—wild gesticulating and him stalking away. The scent of barbecue pulls my attention and Talon jumps in, offering to help with the grill.

The guys that kept their distance when we first arrived begin to approach him. And he's so damn cool. Easygoing and charming. Guys laugh like they've been friends with him for years, and women smile at him with hearts in their eyes.

But I notice how he keeps the conversation at the surface level. I note how he doesn't offer anything about himself, sticking to funny stories that contain no personal details. He doesn't break off into deeper one-on-one conversations with anyone, preferring to flip burgers and address the group at large.

Some people ask him for a selfie, which he poses for easily, even pulling me into a few.

There's music and laughter. Beer and shots of vodka.

And when I look at Talon, there's a tug that doesn't exist with anyone else. There's a connection, an understanding, something more, that causes butterflies to beat their delicate wings in the center of my chest and makes me smile with hearts in my eyes.

When Talon smiles back, I note them in his too.

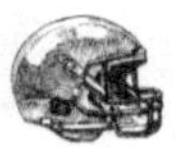

As the night continues, the rowdiness increases. Toby's friends from the boat are wildly drunk, hard liquor flowing through their veins. As a group of women—one I recognize from high school—doubles down on a game of beer pong, they begin to catch up.

Someone starts a bonfire and marshmallows are roasted, squished between graham crackers with chocolate to make s'mores. Sticky fingers and swaying hair, an inky, starlit sky, and the gentle ripple of the lake. Mosquitos are kept at bay by tiki torches and citronella candles. The scent wafts in the air, mixing with beer, perfume, and the heavy tanginess of summertime.

"Have you seen Marlowe?" I ask Talon as he takes a swig of water from a plastic bottle. He nursed a beer for most of the day and swapped his one pint for water when he started barbecuing.

He scans the backyard before shaking his head. "Not for a while."

I tilt my head toward the house, something twisting in my gut. I can't put my finger on what it is but it's strange that I haven't seen her in hours. A few years ago, I would have assumed that she and Toby wandered off to have some alone time, but Toby just shotgunned a beer and is daring a friend to dive off the deck into the lake. What a fucking tool. "I'm going to check on her." I point toward the back entrance of the house, where drunk friends spill out, clinging to each other and laughing hysterically.

For a beat, they remind me of me and Marlowe. Or me and my sister. Nostalgia hits me square in the chest and I wonder if I'll ever have that carefree, live-in-the-moment, giggling hard rush with either of them again.

"I'll come with you," Talon offers.

I place a hand on his chest, feeling his abdomen tighten, muscles clenching, below my fingertips. Damn but is he distracting in the best way possible. "It's okay. I'll be right back."

Talon's jaw clenches, but he nods. "If you don't come back in a few, I'll find you."

I nod, a thrill shooting down my spine at his protectiveness. After months of fearing my boyfriend's anger, it's nice to spend time with a man who is intent on keeping me safe. "I'll be fine."

I move toward the house, weaving through throngs of people on the deck, and push through the back door.

"Jesus," I mutter, taking in the mess that exploded in the kitchen. Various liquor bottles line the counters, caps missing. A stack of Solo cups has tipped over, rolling around the countertops and floor. Pizza boxes are stacked on the island, a few pepperoni slices and crusts discarded beside them. Pools of sticky, sugary substances gather in puddles. I step over a spot on the floor, frowning as I can't discern the type of liquid. It smells rank—like stale beer with an undercurrent of vomit and I cover my nose, gagging into my palm.

"Are you okay?" I ask a woman who stumbles and sways.

She grins at me, her pupils blown.

"I got her," a guy says.

I narrow my eyes at him.

"Kevin! I love you!" she declares, throwing her arms around his neck.

He stumbles as she melts against him but a moment later, he hoists her into his arms. "You need water, Mel," he mutters, moving her onto the deck outside.

Shaking my head, I venture deeper into the house, keeping an eye out for Marlowe. The nautical-themed space, carefully decorated by Toby's mother years ago, when we were in high school, is now dated but clean. Cared for. After this weekend, it looks like a frat party gone wrong and something about it bothers me.

Toby and his friends aren't nineteen-year-old punks anymore, trying to pull one over on his parents without knowing their limits. They're adults—college graduates who should know better. Who should have more respect. Especially Toby considering this is his parents' place and they don't need to let him use it to host parties.

Rolling my eyes, I bend to pick up a handful of empty beer bottles and place them on the coffee table. Knowing Toby, he'll blame Marlowe, and she'll incur his parents' disappointment instead of him.

"I want to leave," Marlowe's voice rings out.

I turn instantly, heading in the direction of her distress.

Down a narrow hallway, past a bedroom and a bathroom, I push into the second bedroom unannounced.

Marlowe's eyes swing to mine. In front of her, her cousin Keller stands, a hand on her elbow. Marlowe's eyes are ringed in red and puffy from crying. Keller looks devastated and tosses an arm around her shoulders, his eyes snapping to mine.

When he sees it's me, he relaxes. "Close the door." He motions toward the door I left ajar, and I nudge it shut.

"Mar, are you okay?" I keep my voice light.

Marlowe looks gutted, like the entire Earth shifted under her feet and she's lost her balance. She lets out a shaky sigh, her knees buckling from whatever she's mentally processing.

Keller shifts forward, catching her before she hits the floor and settling her on the edge of the bed.

"What's going on?" I ask, perching next to her. I wrap an arm around her shoulders, and she leans into me. The second her forehead hits my arm, tears wrack her body. Her upper body trembles form the ferocity of her sobs, but no sounds escape her lips.

"What the hell happened?" My tone is sharp as I wrap my best friend in a tight hug. I look to Keller for answers.

"Jesus," he murmurs, closing his eyes as he hangs his head and grips the back of his neck. When he opens his eyes, they're layered in sadness and shame. "Marlowe," he murmurs, as if waiting for her to clue him in as to what to do, what to say, next.

Marlowe sniffles, sucking in gulps of oxygen. "Tell her. You can tell her." Her voice cracks and she tucks her hair behind her ear. Her cheeks are bright red, but there's a resoluteness in her eyes that wasn't there before.

Keller works a swallow.

"Toby was right. My dad, *Rick*"—there's an edge to her voice now—"isn't my real dad."

I gasp. "What? How do you—?"

The bedroom door snaps open and Toby shadows the doorframe. He glowers, his expression unreadable, his pupils blown. "What the fuck is going on here?" he slurs.

He points between Keller and me, his mouth dropping open.

"Are you going to fuck him, Len? I fucking knew it. All these years, you being a stuck-up, snotty, un-fucking-touchable tease. And now you're gonna give it up to Keller?" He stumbles forward, reaching out a hand to grasp the doorjamb. Anger rolls off his shoulders as he pierces me with dark eyes. "Why not me? I'd make it fucking good for—"

Disgust rolls through me as I stare at him, shocked. My body begins to shake as I process his words.

Un-fucking-touchable tease.

Is that why he's hated me all these years?

Did he ever think something would happen between us? He's my best friend's boyfriend!

I shudder from his words, from the mental picture he painted. From his warped perspective. And then, I realize that he still hasn't noticed Marlowe sitting beside me.

She sucks in a breath and my heart breaks for her.

"Shut the fuck up," Keller says, stepping to Toby.

Behind Toby, I spot a petite blonde. She gasps, ducks her head, and turns away. And the situation worsens.

"Huh?" Toby turns around. "Megan! Wait." He clenches the doorjamb harder as he sways. "We can kick them out. I still call dibs on the bed!"

"Your girlfriend's in there!" Megan hisses, sounding horrified.

Understanding hits me square in the chest and nausea churns in my stomach. Toby was about to hook up with Megan, at Marlowe's birthday party, in his parents' lake house.

"Marlowe?" He narrows his eyes. "She'll understand.

She's so fucking accommodating. Who better than me can she date in our town? No one!" He chuckles to himself.

Marlowe slumps even lower, defeat kicking her down, as my anger swirls. What is wrong with Toby?

He looks too drunk to comprehend what's happening. Instead of apologizing to Marlowe, he glowers at Keller. At me.

"Why're you being such a fucking cockblock?" Toby slurs.

Fury rolls over Keller's expression. His eyes narrow and his mouth twists. "Get the fuck out of here, Toby, before I put you to the fucking ground."

Toby shakes his head, confusion rippling across his face. He spots Marlowe and his eyes widen. "Why're you crying, Mar? I threw you a fucking party. What more do'ya want?"

"Stop talking, Toby," I warn, feeling Marlowe go still beside me. I reach for Marlowe's hand, but her fingers are cold, rigid, in mine. I have no clue how she's processing these bombshells that keep landing in her lap, exploding in her face, and I think she's just starting to shut down.

Toby sneers. "Oh, shit. Leni, you're gonna tell me what to do? Finally back, gracing us with your presence. Why don't you give me whatever you're giving Keller. Or that fucking football player." He grabs his junk obnoxiously.

"That's enough." Keller steps closer, angling his body between Toby and Marlowe and me.

I stand and try to pull Marlowe up beside me, but my friend doesn't move. She doesn't even look up. Her lips mouth silent words and her face is blank, an expressionless mask I hate.

"Fuck you," Toby breathes out heavily. He cocks back his arm, his hand curled into a fist. As he moves forward, he shifts his weight, and throws off his balance. Stumbling forward, his fist comes for me like a freight train.

I throw my hands up, turning my face away, and cower over Marlowe, bracing for the blow that never comes.

Instead, there's a scuffle. Movement of shoes. A cacophony of swear words. And when I raise my head again, Talon's presence eats up the space. His expression is dark and unreadable.

His biceps bunch and the strong planes of his back seem to expand as he hunches over Toby. One hand is wrapped around Toby's throat and his knee is planted in the center of Toby's chest.

His voice is deadly quiet. Even and measured and ice-cold.

Not losing his cool but looking like he could snap at any second.

Toby's face is bright red, his eyes wide. He taps the floor with one hand, but Talon continues to talk. Toby smacks the floor again, more frantic this time, and I start to worry that he can't breathe.

"Dude," Keller murmurs.

Sighing, as if annoyed, Talon loosens his grip. "Look at her again and I'll fucking end you." It's not just a warning, it's a promise. "Speak to her again? I'll draw the process out and make it fucking hurt." And as Talon shifts to his feet and Toby sucks in a lungful of air, everyone in the room knows it.

Keller looks at me. "You okay?"

"Yeah," I say shakily. Adrenaline pools in my mouth and fear shudders through my limbs.

The sound of a bottle of scotch hitting the wall rumbles through my mind.

The skin along my collarbone sears.

The heavy weight of Craig's hand on the back of my neck holds me hostage.

"I'm going to take her home," Keller explains, reaching for his cousin and pulling me from my thoughts.

Marlowe lets Keller support her. She leans on him like a child, nearly clinging to his arm for security.

"I want her to get a good night's sleep and wake up in a familiar place, with family," Keller continues.

"Yeah," I agree, frowning. "She can come home with me."

Keller's eyes hold mine. Years of friendship allow me to understand the gravity of the situation, the concern in his irises. "I know, Len. But she'll have questions, so many questions. And knowing my mom, she'll have answers."

"Right," I murmur. "Do you need anything?"

"Nope. I got her." Keller scoops Marlowe up. She buries her face in his chest, and I run a hand through her hair.

"I'll call you tomorrow, Mar. I love you," I tell her.

Her eyes flicker to mine and a spark of recognition floods her gaze. "Leni."

It's all she says before Keller carries her from the room.

A cold breeze sweeps through with their departure. The door closes behind them and a heaviness—a hot, angry, disbelieving ribbon of tension—settles over the space.

Feeling the wind leave my sails, I plop back down on the edge of the bed.

Talon stands in the corner of the room. His arms are crossed over his chest, his stance wide and imposing. And his eyes—those gray, thundercloud, too-observant irises—are trained on me.

My shoulders slump and I pull in a breath, wondering what I say now.

Before I decide, Talon pushes off the wall and strides toward me. "We're leaving," he says, decisively.

The tension breaks and confusion pours in. *We are?*

He holds out his hand, pulls me up, and leads me from the room.

Apparently, we are. I turn my thoughts off and follow Talon, knowing he'll keep me safe. I trust him.

I barely clock the surprised expressions of the partygoers as Talon leads me out of the lake house. I don't fully inhale or blink or understand anything unfolding around me until I'm settled in the passenger seat of Talon's ride.

He reaches over me, clicking in my seat belt, and places my purse in my lap. Where did he find it?

"I'll be right back," he murmurs, smoothing my hair back from my forehead and dropping a kiss there.

I gasp, looking up at him, but he's already jogging back into the house. He emerges a few minutes later with our weekender bags slung over his shoulders.

He stows them in the trunk, slides behind the wheel, backs out of the driveway, and reaches over the center console.

Talon takes my hand, and I squeeze his fingers, reassurance rolling through me. He's here. I'm safe. Everything is okay.

We drive away from the lake house and in my mind, a metal door clangs closed.

I don't look back.

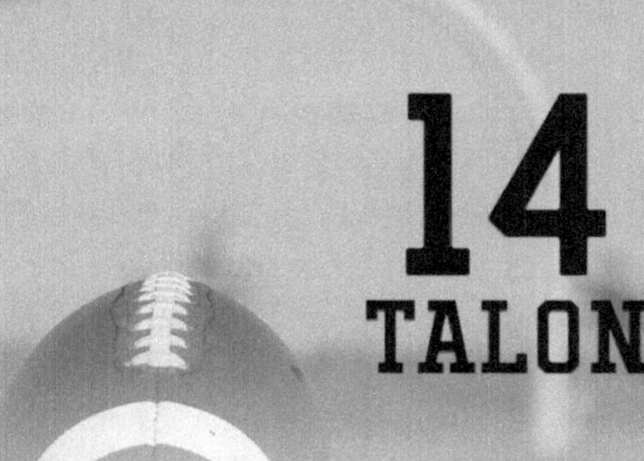

14
TALON

"Two bedrooms," I say, holding up two fingers.

The woman behind the counter of the small, lakefront inn peers at me suspiciously over her glasses. "It's August."

I know. Please have a room available.

"Um, yes, ma'am," I reply, shifting my weight and hitching our weekender bags higher on my shoulder.

Maybe she thinks Leni is my sister? Or a friend.

The woman sighs heavily. She must be close to sixty and the lines in her expression say she's seen it all. And right now, she doesn't love what she's seeing.

Damn. We just need a room.

If I wasn't so worried about Leni, fucking furious over Toby's outburst, and downright exhausted, I'd chuckle at the way the woman is sizing me up. Instead, I'm praying she slides two sets of keys across the desk so I can make sure Leni's okay and tuck her in for the night.

"We've only got one room," she says finally. "And it's the best one." She squints at her computer screen, her eyebrows lifting. "The cost is—"

Beside me, Leni's shoulders slump and she sways. Poor girl is dead on her feet now that the adrenaline has worn off. She's about to crash, hard. Maybe it's better we're in one room so I can keep an eye on her.

"We'll take it." I slide my credit card across the counter

before she can rattle off the price. The only thing I care about right now is making sure Leni is okay.

The woman peers at me again, a frown settling in the corners of her mouth.

For fuck's sake. I fight the urge to roll my eyes. I have no idea what thoughts are running through her mind. I just hope she doesn't recognize me—or Leni—and make this more of a thing than it is.

She harrumphs, runs my card, and hands me a set of keys.

"Thanks," I say, adjusting the bags again. Then, I press a hand to Leni's back, guiding her in the direction of the rooms. "Come on, Len." I feel the woman's eyes, her burning curiosity, between my shoulder blades until we turn the corner.

"We're in room sixteen," I say. Leni doesn't bother responding.

I locate our room, jam the key into the door, and hold it open for Leni.

She enters before me, walks straight to the bed, and sits on the edge. A breath later, she slumps over, resting on her side and curling into herself.

Damn. I am out of my element here.

Dropping the bags to the floor, I kneel at her side, and push some of her beautiful golden hair out of her eyes. "Hey," I say softly.

Leni blinks and I watch as recognition flickers across her face. "Talon."

"Tell me what you need, baby." My concern is through the fucking roof and all I want is to make her feel safe. Protect her so nothing—and no one—can touch her.

"I'm so tired," she whispers.

I stroke her hair. "I know."

Hearing the vile things that spewed from Toby's mouth was enough to set my blood boiling. But when he lifted a hand to Leni, I saw fucking red. I fought through the huddle of people who blocked the doorway, just glimpsing Leni and her blonde hair above the mass of bodies.

And it was the way she shrunk, the way she raised her arms to protect herself, the fear that flashed across her expression, that kicked me in the chest. That caused bile to churn in my stomach.

The silhouette of my mother on the bathroom floor.

The memory came unbidden. It flashed through my mind —clearer than it had any right to be—and in my gut, I knew.

Toby wasn't the first fuckhead to raise a hand to my girl. In the moment, that's how I thought of Leni. That's how I saw her.

And right now, I feel the same.

I won't let anyone hurt a goddamn strand of hair on her head.

But what the fuck happened? Was it the ex—Craig? Is that why she left New York? Or was it someone else—an isolated incident she hasn't been able to speak about?

I want to know every-fucking-thing. But first, I want Leni to know that she's safe. That I'm here. That I'll do whatever the hell she needs.

I reach into my bag and pull out a plastic bottle of water I swiped on my way out of the lake house. "Here, Len. Have some water." I uncap the bottle and hold it to her lips.

She blinks again, her eyes holding mine.

I grip the back of her head and lift it gently. Then, I pour a mouthful of water into her mouth and watch as she sips it. Swallows. Blinks again. "Thank you, Talon. For being here. I —I'm sorry." She sounds so dejected. So…fucking sad. Lost. Nothing like the girl from Coach's stories. Nothing like the woman who whooped my ass in a swimming race. Or the unknowing seductress who cooked dinner for me.

I brush my fingertips over her cheek and lean closer. Resting my forehead to hers, I close my eyes. "Baby, you have nothing to be sorry for."

"I do, Talon," she argues. "I have so many things to apologize for. So many mistakes. So many missed opportunities."

"Tell me what you need. Right now, Leni." I can't do nothing. I need to help her. Be here for her. And I have no clue how.

The sounds of my mother's tears, so fucking long ago, echo. Fresh in my mind. What the hell is happening?

My expression twists and tears—tears I haven't cried in decades—burn the backs of my eyelids.

Someone hurt my girl. The same way someone hurt my mother.

And then, she lost everything. But I won't let that happen to Leni. I won't stand for it.

"I want to shower." She shivers slightly under my touch, and I realize she's cold. Damn, her adrenaline must have plunged. "And put on something warm. And get in bed."

"Okay." I breathe out a sigh of relief. I can do that. "Let's do that." I help her sit up. Keeping one hand anchored to her thigh, I squeeze gently. "I'll go run the water."

She nods and swipes her tongue across her dry bottom lip.

I leave her for a moment, just to flip on the bathroom lights, turn on the showerhead, and make sure the dial is pointed to hot water. I check to see that she has shampoo, conditioner, and body wash. I shake out a towel and hang it on the hook next to the shower, place down a bathmat for when she's done, and move the robe from the back of the door to the top of the vanity.

When I reenter the bedroom, Leni is sitting right where I left her.

Her teeth are chattering now, her eyes nearly closed.

"Come on, Leni," I murmur, stepping in between her legs and bending down. I hook my fingers beneath the hem of her shirt, holding her eyes. "Can I help you?"

In response, she lifts her arms, and I peel the shirt off her frame, discarding it on the bed beside her.

"You got this," I say, to the both of us, as I wrap one arm around her lower back and help her stand. Then, I'm kneeling in front of her, popping the button on her jean shorts, and working them down her thighs.

She's clad in a matching light pink bra and thong set. But other than seeing the color, I don't look. I don't check her out. I keep my focus purely on her well-being. I help her into the bathroom and pull back the shower curtain.

Steam fills the room, turning the mirror hazy.

A sigh of relief falls from Leni's lips. She glances at me over her shoulder. "Will you stay? Wait for me?"

"I'll be right here," I promise.

She nods. "I'm going to…" She trails off, gesturing toward her chest.

"Right." I turn around, giving her a few moments of privacy. When I hear the curtain close, I plop down on the closed toilet seat and wait for Leni to shower.

Her pink underwear and bra are on the floor, and I pick them up, moving them to the vanity next to the robe.

I don't want to put her on the spot, but I want to know what the hell happened tonight. "You okay?" I check in.

"Yes," she replies, her voice stronger than it was a few minutes ago. "I'm almost done."

"Take your time." I wait until she turns the water off.

She pops her head out of the shower and reaches for the towel. Her eyes find mine and a sheepish expression fans across her face. "Thanks for staying with me."

"I'm here for whatever you need," I tell her truthfully.

She ducks back into the shower and a moment later, pushes the curtain open.

The towel is wrapped around her body, one edge tucked into the space between her breasts to keep from falling open. It's short, hitting her mid-thigh. Her blonde hair is darker from the water, falling down her back and clinging to her shoulder blades. Rivulets of water stream down her neck, drip from the ends of her hair, pool into the terrycloth of the towel.

Fuck. I avert my gaze. The last thing I should do is check Leni out. Especially after everything she's been through tonight.

I clear my throat and gesture toward the robe. "I'll step out."

"I'll only be a minute."

I exit the bathroom and suck in a lungful of air. Between the steam, the image of Leni wrapped in a fucking towel, and the high emotions of the last hour, I need a second to pull my shit together.

Raking a hand through my hair, I use this time to pull a pair of sleep shorts and a tank top from my bag. I need to rinse off before I sleep but I want to make sure Leni is settled first.

She steps into the room a moment later, wrapped in the big, fluffy robe.

"You hungry?" I ask.

She shakes her head and yawns. "More tired than anything."

"Right."

She gestures toward the bathroom. "You want to shower?"

"Yeah." I grab a pair of clean boxers from my bag and roll them up along with my pajamas. "You get into bed. I'll crash on the floor and—"

"What?" Leni shakes her head. "Talon, that's ridiculous. It's a king-size bed. It's big enough for both of us."

I shake my head. "I don't want to make you uncomfortable. You had a rough night and—"

"Please," she cuts me off, stepping closer and placing a tentative hand on my arm. "I feel safe with you, Talon. You've never not made me feel safe."

Her words are both a fucking kick to the chest and a healing salve to old wounds all at once.

"Leni…" My voice is tight. So are my fucking balls. I can't sleep beside her when I feel this unsteady.

Angry as fuck over Toby. Worried as hell over her. And so damn curious about what the hell happened in New York.

"Please, Talon," she pleads, her blue eyes bright with unshed tears. "Go shower," she murmurs.

Sighing, I do as she asks. I don't know if I'm capable of not giving into her. From day one, she's been the only woman who's had such a pull over me. Her innocence and her sweetness, at complete odds with the hardness that molded me, have been irresistible.

I take an extra beat in the shower to give her some time to settle into bed and give myself a fucking mental pep talk.

I won't cross any goddamn lines. I'll ensure Leni feels comfortable and safe. I'll be a goddamn gentleman.

Toweling off, I glare at myself in the mirror, mentally swearing to do right by my girl. To hunt down the fucker who first put hands on her and to make sure Toby never lifts a hand in anger against a woman again.

Then, I dress into my pajamas, step into the bedroom, and pray that Leni is asleep.

Her even breathing, followed by a soft snore that pierces the air, assures me she is. I let out a sigh of relief and move to the other side of the bed. I pause for a beat, leaning over to study her in sleep.

She looks like an angel. Her damp hair spreads across the pillow—a halo of dark gold. Long eyelashes, two shades darker than her hair, make half-moons on her high cheekbones. Her full lips are pursed into a rosebud, the tiniest space between them.

She's rolled onto her side, her hands tucked together under her chin, the white duvet pulled up to her shoulders.

"Sunny Leni," I murmur, stroking a hand over her hair. "Sleep well, baby."

Then, I climb into bed beside her, careful to keep space between us, and drop into sleep.

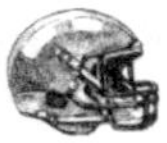

It's nearly four in the morning when she begins to cry out.

"No, no," the whimper falls from her lips, distress lining her face.

"Leni," I murmur, shifting closer and propping myself up on an elbow. "Shh, you're okay."

"Don't hurt me! Stop it! You're hurting me." She throws her hands up to protect her face and my stomach twists in anguish.

"Baby, you're safe. Shh," I try to reassure her, wrapping my arms around her and pulling her closer.

I cradle her head, my palm holding her cheek. The moment her other cheek rests against my chest, her whimpers ease. She snuggles deeper, her eyelids flutter twice, and a sigh falls from her lips.

"Sunny Leni, you're okay, baby. I got you. I won't let anyone hurt you again." I press my lips to the crown of her head, murmuring the sentiments repeatedly as her breathing evens out once more.

She wraps her arms more firmly around me as I continue to soothe her. My voice is calm and quiet. My mind whirls but I don't know what to make of anything. Do I tell Coach? Do I ask Marlowe for more information?

How do I help my Sunny Leni find her sunshine again? The confidence her father always praised and the spark I've witnessed in a handful of moments.

Dragging myself up to rest against the headboard, I settle Leni's frame more firmly over mine. I brush my fingers across her cheek, drag them through her hair, and watch her as she rests. She must be exhausted.

I'm wide awake, my thoughts all over the place.

On the nightstand, Leni's phone buzzes with an incoming text message. I note the screen light before turning my attention back to her.

But then, another text appears. And another.

Is it Coach? Is he worried?

Or Marlowe? Is she in trouble?

When her phone buzzes again, I reach for it.

Leni sleeps soundly and while I'm not crazy about reading her messages, I'm also getting fucking worried.

I pick up her phone.

> Lincoln: Hey! I miss you!

> Lincoln: I know you're going through some things but I'm not going to let you avoid me forever, Len. I love you and you're my sister. Call me, please.

> Keller: Marlowe and I made it home. She's passed out and I'm about to fall asleep too. Thanks for everything tonight, Leni. And thank Talon for me.

> Keller: I'll check in with you tomorrow. Night.

I breathe out a sigh of relief and am about to place her phone back down when another message appears.

This time, my blood runs cold.

> Craig: You can't stay away forever, Leni. I think about you all the time. About what I'm gonna do when I get my hands on you again.

> Craig: Our friends are starting to wonder what happened and you know how I detest lying.

> Craig: You better come back, Leni. Even if I have to drag you back myself.

> Craig: I'm not letting you leave me, baby. You know we belong together.

> Craig: You know you're mine. You understand that, right?

> Craig: Because I love you, Leni. And I don't know what I'll do if you don't come home to me.

> Craig: I don't know what I'm capable of. I don't say that to scare you, baby.

> Craig: I say it because I love you. I'll always love you.

> Craig: And I'm coming to bring you home, sweet Leni.

> Craig: I'm coming for you.

Rage consumes me as I read each message. My vision blurs as anger strums in my veins and horror pounds in my temples.

I clench Leni's phone harder.

That motherfucker.

The ex-boyfriend.

How dare he put his hands on her. How dare he threaten her. How dare he even fucking message her.

I gaze down at the sleeping angel in my arms and know that I'm done for.

I'll cross every line and blow up my entire fucking career to keep her safe. Because the way I feel about her, hell, I don't know what it is but it's something.

And for the first time in a long time, it—she—is the only thing that matters.

"Morning, Sunny Leni." Talon grins as I open my eyes.

"Hey," I say, momentarily confused. I glance around the space of this dated, but clean, bedroom and the events of the night before come rushing back.

Toby and the boat.

Marlowe's concerns.

Keller holding her up.

Toby's hateful, hurtful words.

His fist cocking back.

The scent of scotch.

And Talon.

Talon eating up the space, putting Toby in his place, and getting me out of there.

Taking me here. Helping me shower. Holding me throughout the night.

I'm here. You're safe. I got you.

Talon held me together.

I blink a few times and tuck my hair behind my ears.

I glance at him, and he stares back, his expression expectant, as he perches on the edge of the bed.

"I'm sorry about last night," I manage, my throat scratchy.

He shakes his head, something I can't read flashing in his gray eyes. They're stormy today and yet, his tone is gentle when he adds, "You have nothing to apologize for, babe. Absolutely nothing."

I tilt my head to the side, knowing that's not entirely true. My stomach rumbles loudly and Talon smirks.

"You hungry?"

"Yeah," I admit as my stomach grumbles again. "Starving, actually."

"Come on, let's head into town and get breakfast. Then, we can decide what we're going to do today."

I lift my eyebrows in surprise. "You don't want to head home? Marlowe's birthday bash is a bust." I sigh. "I need to check in with her. And"—I gesture toward him—"it is your day off. You can do whatever you want. You don't have to spend it—"

"There's no one I'd rather spend today with than you," he interjects. "But…" He stands from the bed and grabs a Coyotes Football cap that he drops backwards on his head. "I'd like to spend it doing something fun. So, let's grab a bite and make a game plan."

"A game plan," I repeat. No other words come since I'm too busy ogling Talon. Between the backwards hat, the stubble coating his jaw, and his bunching muscles in the casual tank top he's wearing, my mind blanks. My body stirs to life.

And last night seems like another life entirely. Instead, I want to stay in this one—where I feel safe and at ease in the presence of the sexiest man I've ever spent time with.

Talon grins. "You checking me out, Len?"

I blush but hold his eyes as I admit, "It's kind of hard not to, Talon." I gesture toward him. "I mean, look at you."

"I'd rather look at you," he says smoothly.

I snort and he grins.

"I'm going to grab us some coffees. Give you a chance to dress and do…whatever it is girls do."

I laugh. "Same thing as guys, I'd imagine. But coffee sounds good."

Talon nods and swipes up his keys and phone. "Be back in fifteen."

"Okay. Thanks." I stretch my arms overhead. I remain in bed until the hotel room door closes.

Then, I lean over and grab my phone from the center console. My sister's message makes me smile and for the first time in weeks, I tap out a reply.

> Me: I miss you too, Lincoln. We have a lot to catch up on. I'm sorry I've been such a shitty sister, but I love you for being you and not giving up on me. I'll call you this week. I promise. XO

I pull in a breath after I send it. I owe my sister much more than a phone call but...baby steps.

I read Keller's message next, knowing he's probably still asleep and will give me a ring once he and Marlowe have some answers.

Still, I shoot Marlowe a text letting her know that I love her. I text Mom that I'm doing okay and will be home tomorrow, just so she doesn't worry.

Then, I see Craig's texts and the blood drains from my face.

Why the hell won't he let go? Is he coming here?

I pull in a deep breath and close my eyes. I hate that my intuition for not blocking his number proved true—I need to know if he's going to show up in Knoxville. And right now, I feel like that scenario is more plausible.

I exhale shakily and open my eyes. The swirl of panic doesn't come. The blurry vision and racing heart and inability to drag in oxygen don't occur.

I feel...angry. Frustrated. Exhausted.

But I also feel safe, and I know I have Talon to thank for that. Not that he knows it. Not that he'll ever know it.

Flipping off the duvet, I stand from the bed and stretch again. The least I can do is make sure he enjoys his day off. Talon's been nothing but good to me, and last night he went above and beyond, showing up for me and my friend. Today, I'm game for whatever he wants to get into, and I'll make sure we have a great time.

Maybe I'm just distracting myself from my reality but right now, I want the distraction. I want a break from the tumultuous feelings of the past twenty-four hours. I want to have some fun with Talon and live in that reality for a minute.

My mind made up, I stride to my weekender bag, dig out my toiletries, and enter the bathroom. Then, I fix my hair, apply some makeup, and dress for the day.

By the time Talon returns with our coffees, I'm ready to go. And I love the double take he does when he sees me.

Today is going to be better than good. It's going to be the day I start taking back pieces of my life. Of myself. And I'm not sure if I'd have the courage to do so without Talon by my side.

"Do you have an idea what you want to do on your day off?" I ask as I shovel a forkful of scrambled eggs into my mouth.

His eyes brighten and he nods, polishing off his second pancake. "I do."

I lean forward, lifting an eyebrow.

"There's a water park ten minutes from here," he announces, sounding like a teenager on the first day of summer vacation.

A bubble of laughter erupts. "Seriously?"

Talon nods, the grin never falling from his face.

"Wow, I haven't been to a water park in...years." My forehead crumples as I try to recall how many years it's been. "Since high school with Lincoln," I decide.

"Well, I haven't been since last summer, but water parks are my favorite so..." Talon trails off.

"I'd love to go to a water park."

"Good," he says, starting in on his third pancake. "They're kind of my thing."

I snort. "You're thing?"

He nods, his eyes dancing. "I went once as a kid. I must have been in fifth or sixth grade. My foster parents—Allen and Kim, probably the best I ever had—had a biological son, Frankie. It was Frankie's birthday, and he invited a handful of friends and me. It was one of the best days of my life." Talon's eyes take on a faraway look, as if recalling that day. His smile never slips. "I loved every ride I went on—but the free fall. Man, that was wild." He chuckles. "Ever since then, I've made it a point to hit as many water parks as I can."

"How many have you been to?" I wonder.

He snorts. "At least three hundred."

"Three hundred!" I narrow my eyes. Is he fibbing?

Talon nods enthusiastically. "That's one of my bucket list items."

"Go to as many water parks as possible?"

"Go to a major water park in every state. A few years ago, when I was in college, one of my teammates invited me to his hometown in Wisconsin. It was close to Noah's Ark water park. That was sick. The town is even called the Water Park Capital of the World."

"Stop it!" I laugh, loving this side of Talon. The amused, playful guy with more personal insights than he usually offers. It's like peeking behind a curtain I've been wondering about for ages.

And I am thrilled by everything he shares with me.

"What else is on your bucket list?" I wonder.

He shakes his head and takes a bite of bacon. "It's not as elaborate as yours. But maybe it should be. Spending time with you, Leni, has got me thinking."

"About what?"

"Just, life. I've never really traveled, you know? I've never thought about places to see or things to experience. For so long, it was all about football. Get a scholarship, keep the scholarship, then get drafted. Earn a good deal. Keep my position on the roster. I don't know anything but hustling to stay in the game. The only time I ever really took off was when my mom passed and to be honest, if it wasn't for your dad stepping in, I don't know if I would have had as much time with her as I did."

"My dad really helped you with all that?"

"He did," Talon confirms.

"I'm not surprised," I offer. "It's just that, he's never said anything."

"He's a stand-up guy."

"Yeah," I agree. "It's funny, you know, for years, I never really thought of my parents as having big identities, relationships and lives, outside of being Lincoln's and my mom and dad."

Talon eyes me curiously. "I don't know about that." His response is honest, his tone thoughtful. "But I imagine you and Lincoln don't share everything with your parents either. And I'm sure they know your lives are fuller than only being their children."

"Yeah," I say softly, wondering again if I should have confided in them sooner. What would I say? What would they do?

"You're lucky, Leni. I don't know many men who love their kids the way your dad loves you and Lincoln." He eyes me again, this time more seriously. As if he's trying to relay more than he's letting on.

I frown and Talon clears this throat.

"You know," he continues, gesturing for me to keep eating. I manage another two bites. "When my mom was in the hospital, Coach came and sat with me a lot of nights. That's when he talked about your family, shared stories about you and your sister." He grins wickedly and I groan.

"What did he say?"

Talon snorts. "I'm not gonna betray the man's trust, Len."

"Oh, God. Embarrassing stories, weren't they?"

"Adorable," Talon replies. "I loved hearing everything he shared about you. It was during that time—one of the darkest of my life—that I started to think of you as pure sunshine."

His admission pulls me up short and I place down my fork. "You mean…?"

"Meeting you was a long time coming," he says by way of explanation. "But you helped me through a rough time in my life. And you don't even know it." He sighs, wiping his mouth with a napkin. Then, he fixes me with a steely gaze. "If there's anything I can ever help you with…" A raised eyebrow. "I'm here, Len."

Another cryptic message. Is this about last night? About Toby and Marlowe?

Or, my heart begins to race, did he see Craig's text messages? Does Talon know?

I mumble my thanks, and he resumes eating as if he hasn't just made me question things.

Am I reading into things?

Shaking my head, I take a sip of coffee.

"Tell me more about the debutante ball. When's the big day?" Talon asks. His expression is open and eager, throwing me for another loop.

I must be reading into things. That's it. My nerves haven't fully settled after the past twenty-four hours.

"Well, it's the twenty-first of September. It's usually held in June but the regular head organizer, Mrs. Tipton, is pregnant. Due to the complications she faced and the need to reshuffle the committee to various tasks, the committee decided to delay the ball. But it's coming along. I'm excited about it and to be involved in it. Marlowe's sister Adi is one of the participants."

"Really?" Talon seems genuinely curious, so I continue to fill him in on plans for the event—the menu, the first waltz, the signature drink.

By the time I finish talking, he's flagging the server down for the check. And then, we head to the water park for a carefree, fun afternoon.

Another thing I haven't experienced in ages. Another thing I wouldn't want to share with anyone more than Talon Miller.

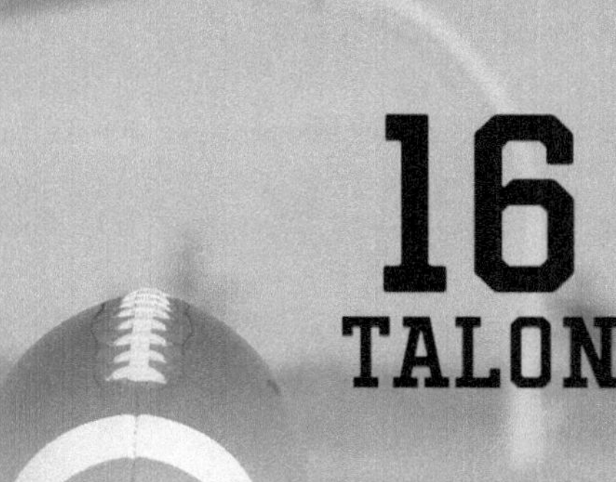

16
TALON

Leni Strauss in a bikini should be illegal.

In fact, witnessing the number of men who do double takes—some of them while with their own women—is alarming. Of course, Sunny Leni is completely oblivious, bouncing on her tippy toes and pointing to one slide or another.

But I clock every second glance. Every look that lingers too damn long. And even two whistles.

The interest Leni generates has me shadowing her every move. And even though I know I'm being overbearing, she doesn't seem to mind. Instead, she latches onto my arm, gives me more of those sunny smiles, and races me to the top of every ride.

"This one! The free fall is next!" she exclaims, tugging me toward the water park ride that made me a lover of water parks.

And it's funny, because it's obviously not a big thing, but I love sharing this day with her. For years, I'd hit a water park and bring along one of my teammates who expressed an interest. And yeah, we always had fun.

But today is different. Today is special and it warms me from the inside out, like rays of sunshine that I haven't felt since that first trip when I was about twelve.

Leni and I make it to the top of the slide, and I glance down.

I hear her suck in a breath, and I glance at her over my shoulder.

She meets my eyes and a slow smile spreads across her beautiful face.

"You ready, Sunshine?" I ask.

"After you, Miller."

I snort. "You sure? Ladies first?"

"Y'all can go together. There are two slides," the lifeguard offers.

I raise an eyebrow. Leni's smile widens, and we each take our place.

"On three," I say.

"I'll see you at the bottom," she replies.

"Yeah, I'll get there first."

Leni snickers.

"Three," I start. "Two."

And then I whoop with glee as Leni takes off—being a sneaky, little cheater.

"Leni!" I holler after her, pushing myself down the slide.

My heart soars up into my throat and my stomach plummets to my toes. For a heartbeat, I'm weightless.

I'm not the kid with a chip on his shoulder. I'm not the life of every party, just to be included. For a beat, I'm just Talon, a guy free-falling for the prettiest, sweetest, sunniest woman I've ever laid eyes on.

When I reach the bottom, the slide bottoms out and the water splashes up.

Leni's already waiting on the side. "Beat ya."

"You're a fucking cheater." I laugh.

She smirks. "That was some free fall."

"Yeah," I say, getting lost in those cerulean eyes. "It was."

We spend the rest of the afternoon in the lazy river. I drink a beer, she sips a mojito, and we talk about everything and nothing.

Football and event planning.

She tells me how one day, she wants to be a wedding planner and I can see it. Easily.

I tell her I'm happy she's home and I mean it. Her being here has changed the game for me. I just don't know how yet.

Because while I've dropped some breadcrumbs, hoping she'll open up and tell me about Craig, about New York, about the real reason she's back in Tennessee, she hasn't said a word.

Instead, I've gotten her bright blue eyes. Her laughter and her light.

By the time we arrive back at the hotel, I realize I'm smitten.

And I want it all with Leni Strauss.

The good, the bad, and the ugly.

"Want to go out for dinner?" I ask after she blow-dries her hair.

"Honestly, I'm pretty beat. Want to order room service?"

"Sure," I agree.

Leni grins and flops back on the bed. "I wish we didn't have to go home tomorrow."

"This was a pretty epic escape."

"Did you have a good day off?" she asks, propping herself up on an elbow.

"The best day," I agree, taking a seat next to her. The bed dips under my weight.

Leni's wearing a linen, white button-down shirt with a plunging neckline and short cotton shorts. She looks comfortable and at ease.

Meanwhile, I'm starting to feel like the clock is running down.

It's been a whirlwind of a weekend and even though it's

only two days, I feel like so much has transpired between us. I've finally admitted that the way I feel about Coach's daughter is legit. I'm not willing to squander it, and I know I need to come clean about my feelings to Leni.

But I want her to trust me back. I want her to confide in me. I want her to tell me about Craig.

And still, she hasn't uttered a word.

If we return to Knoxville tomorrow without addressing this unknown elephant in the room, what will happen? Will we continue to skirt around each other?

I fucking hate that, especially after spending these endless hours with her. Hell, I held her throughout the night. I can't exactly pretend that shit didn't happen. Or worse, doesn't mean anything.

"I'm going to call an order in," she says, scanning the menu. "What are you in the mood for?"

"A burger and fries," I say, rattling off my go-to room service order.

She calls in our dinner. After hanging up, she turns to me and asks, "Now what?"

And that's my cue.

Sighing, I decide to lay it all out.

"I had fun today, Leni."

"Me too," she says. But something about my tone must clue her in that I'm gearing up for a serious conversation. She straightens on the bed, resting her back against the pillows.

"I saw your phone last night," I admit. "I read the messages from Craig."

"I..." She stops, frowning. "You read my—"

"I got worried it was your parents. Or Marlowe. You had just cried out in your sleep from a nightmare," I explain. "I didn't want to wake you, so I thought I'd just make sure Marlowe was okay. It was a text from your sister and then, Keller. I was about to put your phone down when all the messages from Craig started coming through. One right after another."

Her brow furrows, her lips part. But it's not betrayal that streaks across her face. Betrayal, or anger, I was prepared for.

Instead, it's shame. And that twists me up pretty damn good.

"He was probably drunk," she confesses quietly.

"How often does he message you?" I keep my voice low.

"Too often," she replies. "But I haven't answered any of them. Not a single one."

I nod, holding her gaze with mine. "What happened in New York, Len? Why'd you really come home?"

Tears well up in Leni's eyes and she closes them. One tear falls and slides slowly down her cheek as she gathers her thoughts.

I thought she'd put up a fight. Yell at me, push me away.

Instead, she looks devastated. Fucking gutted and I hate that for her.

I reach out tentatively to brush away her tear. Before I drop my hand, she grasps it and holds on tightly.

"I had to leave," her voice cracks.

"I'm glad you did." I move closer to her. "You can tell me anything, babe. I'm not going to judge you. I'm on your team. I just want to keep you safe, and Len, those messages aren't nothing. Not if you had to leave."

"I know," she admits.

"Did he put his hands on you?" There's an edge to my voice I can't conceal, and I don't fucking care. I don't want to scare Leni but at the same time, the thoughts I'm conjuring are torturous. I need to know the truth. I need to know what I'm up against.

"Yes," she whispers.

"Did you ever press charges?"

She shakes her head, more tears tracking her cheeks.

"He ever…" Fuck, I don't even know how to say it. "Take more than you were offering?"

She stares at me for a beat, her eyes widening in horror. "No, no, never." She shakes her head vehemently and a tiny flicker of relief infiltrates my chest.

Small fucking miracles.

"He would just get angry sometimes. Throw a bottle of scotch. Smack or pinch me. Only once it was really bad."

"It's never an only, Leni," I whisper.

"I know," she admits miserably.

"What happened?"

"He…" She stops and her shoulders shake.

"It's okay, baby." I place a reassuring hand on her knee.

She shakes her head again, whether to refute my words or clear her mind, I don't know. "He choked me. Left marks on my collarbone. And the next morning, I called my mom."

"Fuck, my sunshine," I say, feeling sick. I tug her closer, hoping it's okay. Thank God she comes willingly, and I wrap her in my arms, hugging her against my chest. "Leni, I'm so fucking sorry."

"Don't be. It's my—"

"Don't say it," I warn. "Don't say it's your fault."

"I should have left, Talon. I should have left him weeks before I did. I just kept thinking if I could…be better, change…it would be fine. But instead, it kept getting worse."

"How long did you stay?"

"Almost two years," she whispers.

I close my eyes, feeling the blood drain from my face. Fuck. I don't want to press her too hard, but I can't stop the awful thoughts that roll around my mind. "Was he violent from the start?"

Leni shudders in my arms. "It started after six months. It was a slow build—he became increasingly controlling. A comment one day, a moment of anger weeks later." She shakes her head. "I know how it sounds, Talon, but when you're in it…there are things you choose not to see. Or admit to yourself."

She breaks my fucking heart. I lock down my emotions so I don't scare her. More than anything, I want Leni to know she can confide in me. Kissing the top of her head, I murmur, "You're safe now, Leni. You're here. Home."

"I know," she sobs. "Marlowe said the same thing."

"So, you talked to Marlowe?" The thought is mildly reassuring. It means she's starting to come to terms with things. She's beginning to confide in others.

"Yeah. Something similar recently happened in her family and…" She shakes her head. "She's my best friend. We were both keeping secrets, but it was me who put all the distance between us. I did the same with Mom and Dad. With Lincoln."

I blow out an exhale. "Your family and friends love you, Leni. More than anything in the world. They will understand. We're all on your side. But we gotta protect you, babe. I need to keep you safe."

She nods, her eyes holding mine even as more tears fall. "I feel safe when I'm with you, Talon. Right from the beginning."

I brush away more tears. "I'm glad. It would kill me if you didn't because Len, more than anything, I want to protect you. The way I feel about you… I've never felt this way before."

"Ever?"

I shake my head. "Last night, when I saw you throw your hands up to avoid Toby's fist, it was like a fucking wake-up call. I remembered my mom. I mean, I was only a kid and still, that image, that memory, lingers. I've never stood by when a man, any fucking man, got rough with a woman. But last night… Leni, I could have fucking killed him."

"I'm sorry I put you in that position," she murmurs, sounding horrified.

"No, baby. Don't you see? You mean so much to me. I'd do anything for you. And these feelings, the intensity of them, it's new for me. I'm blurring every goddamn line and, Len, I don't care. I care about you and your safety. Your happiness. I don't want you to carry around shame or guilt or whatever. I want you to find your sunshine again and I want to help you do it."

Leni sucks in a breath and then she leans forward and presses her mouth to mine.

I taste Talon's surprise as I kiss him. I know I'm throwing a lot at him but God, do I want—no need—this man to remind me that I'm not broken.

I am worthy. I am enough.

And his words—God, those words saved a part of my soul.

I'm blurring every goddamn line and, Len, I don't care. I care about you and your safety. Your happiness. I don't want you to carry around shame or guilt or whatever. I want you to find your sunshine again and I want to help you do it.

I shift closer and as I deepen our kiss, Talon wakes up. His hand cups my cheek as he kisses me back. Tentatively, sweet and soft at first. And then harder, with an edge.

"Len…" He breaks away, resting his forehead against mine. "Baby, we—"

"Please, Talon." I don't even care how needy I sound. For months, I've been questioning myself. For weeks, I've been mentally berating myself. And now, I've worked up the courage to confide in this man and he…he gave me unconditional grace. He gave me his love and light.

He gave me himself. And I want all of him.

"I need you," I admit.

His eyes flash. They darken. And then, they smolder—all intensity and desire.

"Leni, you just admitted some really heavy things. Maybe—"

"I know what I want, Talon," I cut him off, understanding his line of thinking. Loving him more for it. But… "This isn't a desperate, throw caution-to-the-wind decision. I've wanted you for weeks. We've been skirting around it but, Talon, the feelings I have for you, they're real. You've healed parts of me you don't know about. And I want this. I want you."

"Christ." He sounds physically pained. He rolls his lips together as I run my fingers across the scruff of his jawline. His breath hitches and his hold on my side tightens. "If we do this, Leni, it's real. I won't be able to walk away. Or pretend it was a weekend thing. Or hide us from your father and the team. You're the only woman I've ever had these feelings for, and I've been in the game a long fucking time, baby. Either this is real, or we're just friends. No matter what, I'll always have your back. I'll help you through whatever comes next. But baby, this doesn't just blur a line. It crosses it completely."

It's exactly what I hoped he'd say. Still, hearing him voice his want for me—for real—causes relief and hope to roll through my body. Talon's assurances mix with the desire already sparking to life. "I want to cross every line with you," I admit.

He breathes out, his eyes holding mine.

A knock at the door sounds. "Room service."

Talon snorts and shakes his head, starting to shift off the bed.

"Leave it," I say, not wanting anything to interrupt this moment. "I want you, Talon." I look right into his eyes when I say it. "I wasn't a girl who cowered. I used to know what I wanted and asked for it. The version of myself I became… I'm not proud of it. But I'm finding my way again and you've been a big part of that. I know how I feel about you. I know what I want with you. I want this." I gesture between us before dropping my hand to his thigh.

"Room service." Another knock on the door.

"I'll be right there; you can leave it," Talon calls out.

I grin, biting my bottom lip.

He shakes his head. "You're going to be the end of me, Leni."

And then, we both move forward, meet in the middle, our lips crashing together. I move up onto my knees as Talon's arms wrap around my middle, one hand landing in the center of my back to anchor me to him. As he pulls me closer, my breasts flatten against his chest and the contact alone is stimulating. It's been so long since I've been able to free-fall into a feeling, a moment, with a man and not be afraid.

As I reclaim parts of myself, giddiness strums through me. I kiss Talon deeply and he meets me eagerly, our tongues caressing and discovering each other. He tastes like mint and summer and hope.

My hands grip the hem of his shirt. I pull it up his body slowly, leaning back to appreciate the muscles that ripple underneath. Washboard abs, a toned torso, perfect pecs. His shirt clears his head and then, his strong arms close around me again, pushing me onto my back as he covers my body with his.

I laugh.

He grins. "Is this okay?" His voice is soft.

"More than okay." I wrap my legs around his waist and hook my right ankle over my left foot.

"If anything doesn't feel good or isn't what you want, what you like—"

"I'll tell you," I promise.

He holds my eyes for a beat, as if gauging the sincerity of my declaration. Then, he lowers his mouth to mine and kisses me again. Deeply and passionately.

Talon's hands slide up my body, underneath the thin material of my button-down. One hand covers the cup of my bra and squeezes my breast playfully before tugging it down to roll my nipple between his fingers. I gasp, arching into him.

His tongue dives into my mouth as my core rubs against his growing erection.

And fuck, does it feel good. I whimper from the contact alone, slowly grinding against him.

He hisses and then rolls to the side, one of his large hands traveling down my body, before slipping into my panties. His fingers part me and I moan.

"Fuck, Leni, you're soaked." His voice deepens.

I clutch his forearm, as if to keep his hand between my legs. I need the contact, the friction, the release.

"How long has it been?" Talon presses as his fingers drag through my folds before starting to circle my clit.

"Too long," I practically pant.

"Fuck, baby." He kisses me hard.

And then, I feel him everywhere. His mouth at my ear, his lips on my neck. His hand on my breast, one between my thighs. He travels down my body slowly, taking time to push my shirt all the way up, over my breasts. They're trussed up on top of the cups of my bra and I'm too damn turned on to care how I look one way or another.

Talon peels my shorts and panties down my legs and discards them. His knees hit the floor, and he tugs my legs to the edge of the bed, tossing them over his shoulders.

"Fuck, your pussy is so damn pretty, baby. Glistening for me like this," he growls, his eyes drinking me in.

"Talon," I whimper.

"Tell me you want this, Leni."

"I want it so badly," I admit, my eyes watching him as he takes his fill. Then, he braces his forearms on either side of my thighs, dips his head, and drags his tongue over my core.

I buck against him, the contact too much. Too damn good.

Talon begins to lick and suck, his tongue swirling around my clit. He pushes a finger inside and I gasp. Before I fully adjust, he adds a second finger, and my eyes nearly roll back in my head. The fullness stretches me deliciously. That, coupled with how he laps at my clit, drives me wild.

Talon thoroughly consumes me.

Higher and higher. My body responds to his touches instantly.

But it's the mental freedom. The clarity. The desire that has no strings attached that drives me over the edge.

"Talon!" I cry out his name.

He responds by quickening the pace of his fingers and sucking so damn hard on my clit, I can hear my arousal smack against his lips.

I come for him. Hard and fast and desperately.

"Oh, God," I breathe out, my hand reaching down.

He grabs my fingers and holds. "Christ, but you're fucking gorgeous."

I chuckle, the sound filled with awe. "I've never… God, it's been so long."

Talon crawls up my frame. "I love that I can make you feel good, Leni."

I wrap my legs around his waist again. "I want to make you feel good, too."

He smirks and brushes my hair back from my face. "There's no rush, baby."

And I love how he gives me an out. Makes this about me and my needs. But doesn't he realize how much I need him?

"I'm not rushing it. I want you," I repeat.

Something that looks a lot like hope shimmers in his gaze as he lowers his head and kisses me hard. I taste myself on his lips and moan into his mouth.

"So fucking sweet," he says, lining up at my entrance. Then, he pauses. "Fuck, babe. I don't have a condom."

"I'm on birth control. The shot," I explain.

Talon lets out a shaky breath.

I tilt my pelvis up, dragging my swollen pussy against his rock-hard erection.

He moans, his eyes dropping to half-mast.

"I'm clean," I assure him. "I got tested…after."

"I'm clean too," he says, forcing his eyes to meet mine. "And I don't ever mess around without a condom."

Shit. I nod, dropping my ass back to the bed. "I understand. I—"

His hands find my hips and he squeezes. "I didn't mean you, Leni. I fucking want this. I just want to make sure—"

"I'm sure."

The muscle in his jaw tics once. "Fuck me," he growls before kissing me hard. Then, he enters me on a sharp thrust, and I cry out in pleasure, turning my head to the side.

Talon slides all the way home, and then holds himself still so I can adjust to his size. Which is extra fucking large. But it feels incredible. Powerful.

He pulls out slowly before entering me again. Our eyes hold and I note the awe that shimmers in his irises. Warmth spreads through my limbs and a calmness I've never experienced before follows. I slide my palm across his cheek, the edges of my fingers disappearing into his dark hair. He leans into my touch and it's involuntary. Natural.

Time stands still and peace consumes me. Talon dips his mouth to brush his lips across mine and I melt. With Talon, I feel complete in a way I never have with a man before.

Worthy and enough. Whole.

His body shields mine; his arms bracket me into a little cocoon, and lying beneath him, I feel so safe and taken care of that tears prick my eyes.

"Leni," he murmurs, concern shadowing his eyes.

"I don't deserve you, Talon."

Talon snorts and brushes his lips softly against mine. "No, Sunshine. It's me who doesn't deserve you. But fuck if I'm not going to try."

Then, he sets a rhythmic pace, and our bodies come together, finally catching up to our minds. Our hearts.

We come apart at the seams simultaneously. And in that moment, we come together too.

"This is the best cold hamburger I've ever had," Talon says as we sit in bed, our dinner spread out around us, and watch reruns on television.

I laugh, popping a lukewarm fry in my mouth. "I'm fuller than I've been in a long time."

Talon snickers, catching my double entendre. "Good." He pinches my side. "You need to eat, baby. And I intend to feed you every chance I get."

I roll my eyes and take a sip of my Coke.

We hang out the rest of the evening and it's normal. Easy.

We eat and talk. Watch television and snuggle.

I fall asleep in my button-down shirt and panties. Talon stretches out beside me in his boxers. Sometime during the night, he wraps his arms around me and tugs me against his chest.

And I sleep soundly. No nightmares, no fear.

It's the best sleep I've had in over a year.

When I wake in the morning, I look directly into Talon's heather gray eyes. "Did all of that really happen?"

He smiles. "Yeah. And it's just the beginning, Leni."

I drive back to Knoxville with my hand in Leni's. The scent of her perfume wraps around us, and memories from last night roll through my mind.

This weekend was life-changing.

I glance over at her. She stares out the window, lost in thought. Music plays through the speakers, and the silence between us is comfortable.

The awkward shit is done. We've moved past it.

Relief flows through my limbs and I grin.

As if sensing my gaze on her, Leni turns and catches my eyes. She smiles back.

"What are you thinking about?" I ask.

She blushes and bites her bottom lip. "Last night."

My smirk widens as I turn my eyes back to the road. "Which part?"

"All of it. But mostly, when can we do it again?"

I snort. "Tonight, I hope?"

Leni nods slowly. "My dad—"

"Don't worry about your dad, baby. I'm going to talk to him."

Leni is quiet and I glance at her.

"You're worried?" I guess.

She sighs. "Yeah. I'm not sure how he's going to take it."

Disappointment churns in my stomach, chasing away my

good vibes from last night. But I shouldn't be surprised. "Because I'm a football player?"

She shakes her head. "Because I've been lying to him and Mom for months."

My disappointment morphs into pride as I process Leni's words. "You're going to talk to them, Leni? Really?"

She manages a watery smile. "I want to, Talon. God, I'm scared."

I squeeze her hand. "Why? Your parents are two of the best, most understanding people I know. They'll want to know the truth."

"I don't doubt that," she agrees. "It's more that…I'm so disappointed in myself. For staying with Craig, for making excuses. My parents didn't raise me to be a coward."

"You're not—"

She shakes her head. "I meant the part about lying to them. I've let it go on for so long and now, I feel like I've let them down as much as I have myself." Leni rolls her lips together and shrugs. "I don't want to tell them that."

"Len," I breathe out. "We'll play this however you want. I'm here for you. But your parents will never not show up for you, baby. And I just can't look your dad in the eyes and lie to him. About the way I feel for you," I clarify.

She nods. "Would it be okay if we tell them about us first? And then, I'll ease them into learning more about what happened with Craig?"

"Of course."

"It means my dad's anger…" She trails off, blowing out a breath. "I don't want you to bear the brunt of his frustration. It's not fair to you."

I shake my head ruefully at her concern. I've never had anyone look out for me like this before. I like it, but I don't want her worrying about that shit. "Don't stress it, Leni. I can take it."

Relief filters through her blue eyes. "Thank you, Talon."

"Whatever you need," I remind her.

We drive the rest of the way in comfortable silence, listening to music and chatting. She tells me more about Marlowe and her concerns for her friend. She explains how much she misses her sister and is going to call Lincoln. She admits how much she loved this weekend.

I listen eagerly, wanting her every thought. I'm still riding the natural high of last night. And then again, this morning.

Getting lost in Leni is easy and for the first time, I understand what Cohen and West went through last season. The way their entire worlds flipped overnight.

It's something you can't understand until it happens to you. Until those feelings hit you straight on and change everything. The weird thing is, you crave it more than you fear it. And then, you know it's the real deal.

Leni is the real fucking deal. So much so, I'm going to man up and tell Coach Strauss about us. I would never do that—risk my relationship with him and the team—if I wasn't one-hundred percent certain Leni is it for me.

But I've been on my own a long time. The fact that this is the first time I've ever felt this way is more than telling. It's everything and I won't risk my pride or position on the team for what could very well be my once-in-a-lifetime. I've watched teammates make that mistake too many times.

While I didn't fully understand what was at stake at the time, I do now. I'm not risking a real shot, a real future, with Leni when it's staring me straight in the face.

When we arrive at Leni's house, I pull in the driveway and kill the engine.

She takes a deep breath. "You sure about this?"

"Positive."

She turns to me. "I don't want you to feel like you're jeopardizing your career or position with the team for...this." She gestures between us. "It's new and—"

"I know how I feel about you, Len." I need her to trust my

instincts the same way I do. "And I admire your dad too much to sneak around. He's the type of man I want to grow into. What would he do?" I quirk an eyebrow, already knowing the answer.

Leni sighs. "The same as you. He had to fight for my mom's hand in marriage. He was a German immigrant, and she was from old Southern money. There were different expectations set for her."

"And?" I press, wanting to know how the story unfolded.

"He didn't back down and eventually, my granddaddy respected him for it."

I smirk. "You just proved my point."

"But it wasn't easy, Talon. For years, my mom's parents didn't accept Dad. They gave him—both of them—a hard time."

"Nothing has ever come easy to me, Len. To be honest, if it did, I wouldn't want it. Wouldn't trust it."

"Okay," she breathes out, looking worried.

For a moment, nerves rattle through me. "This is what you want, right?" Shit, am I reading this wrong? Am I moving too fast, expecting things from Leni that she's not ready to commit to? It's easy to want something in the heat of a moment. It's something different to admit to it the following day.

Her eyes widen and panic flickers over her expression. "More than anything," she breathes out. "I guess it's just, more than I expected. You're more than I ever hoped for."

I shake my head, cupping her cheek affectionately. More than anything, I want to lean over the console and kiss her. But first, I want to man up and come clean with Coach.

As much as I want his blessing, want to earn his respect, I'm not willing to walk away from Leni regardless of what he says. It's a scary realization.

For years, I lived and died by the unspoken rules of my

football team. Now, I'll break them all to take my shot with Leni.

She gives me that sunny smile I love, and we exit the SUV.

Rolling back my shoulders, I walk to her parents' front door and wait for her to let us inside.

We're in the foyer for about twenty seconds before Coach and Vicki round the corner. Coach's expression is guarded while Vicki's is hopeful.

I pull in a settling breath and hold out a hand to Coach.

He shakes it, his grip firm, his eyes searching mine. "How was the weekend?"

Leni sighs and tilts her head toward the living room. "We should talk."

"About what?" Vicki asks, sounding worried.

"Well, for starters, Marlowe," Leni admits.

That seems to relax her parents slightly. We follow her into the living room.

"Would you like something to drink, Talon? Or to eat? Are you guys hungry?" Vicki's eyes dart between Leni and me.

"I'm fine," Leni says.

"All good, Vicki. Thank you," I reply.

"What happened with Marlowe?" Coach frowns.

Vicki pitches forward in her seat and I note the worry in her expression. The Strausses are such good people. It's hard to imagine families like them exist. Could I ever have that one day? Will they ever fully accept me?

I hope so. I temper down the feelings that rise in my chest and turn my attention to Leni's explanation as she fills her parents in.

She tells them about Toby and the boat.

About the rumors of Marlowe's biological father.

At this, Coach swears, and Vicki clasps a hand over her mouth.

But then, Leni starts to paint the picture of Toby losing his cool, raising his fist to her and Keller.

Coach is on his feet when Leni says, "And then, Talon put him on the ground."

Coach whirls around, pinning me with his gaze. "You good?"

I hold up my hands. "I'm fine. We…we left the lake house and checked into a hotel for the rest of the weekend."

Coach frowns. Vicki's eyes ping pong from Leni to me to Coach and back to me. Understanding dawns on her expression but Coach still looks confused.

"Why didn't you come home?" Coach asks Leni.

She looks to me helplessly and I realize this is it. This is the moment.

"I have feelings for your daughter, Coach." I man up, say the words, and lay it on the line.

Vicki sniffles and it's a punch to the gut. Is she horrified?

But when I glance at her, she doesn't look horrified. She looks like she's trying to get a handle on…happy feelings.

Coach's eyes narrow, his expression twisting harshly. "Excuse me?" he snaps. "What the fuck did you just say to me?"

"I have feelings for Leni, sir. Real feelings," I repeat.

Coach gapes at me. "Leni, go to your room." He points toward the hallway without ever looking her way.

"Friedrich," Vicki murmurs.

"Daddy," Leni says, moving closer to me and lacing our hands together. "I'm an adult. I don't need your permission to date—"

"My house, my rules," he growls.

Vicki shakes her head.

"Fine!" Leni throws a hand in the air. "I'll just move in with Talon then."

Shit. My thoughts scatter and nerves zip through my chest as the situation deteriorates. I keep a firm grip on Leni's hand though. Because the one thing I'm not losing today is her.

"Coach," I say, holding his eyes. "I respect you more than

any other man I know. I'm not saying this as a fleeting thing. You know me, and I hope you know my character. I've never had a serious relationship before."

"Trust me, I know," he interjects.

Vicki stands beside him and places a warning touch on his forearm. "Keep going, Talon," she says, not unkindly.

"Leni's it for me, sir. I didn't expect this to happen, but it did and I'm not asking for your blessing, either. I'm telling you, man to man, because I admire the hell out of you. I'm falling for Leni."

"It's been one weekend," he seethes, holding up a finger.

"It's been brewing longer than that," I admit.

"You just got out of a relationship," he accuses his daughter. "Is this…a rebound?" He gestures between us.

Damn. That fucking hurt.

"Friedrich!" Vicki hisses.

"What?" He glares at her. Then, back at me. "No, no. I don't accept this. Leni, get up to your room. Talon, get the hell out of my house." Then he stalks from the room. The back door slams closed a moment later, and I wince.

"He'll calm down," Vicki says by way of apology.

Beside me, Leni rolls her eyes but, like her mother, doesn't seem to take her father's reaction seriously.

"Come on, I'll walk you out." She tugs on my arm.

I stand beside her, bewildered and unsure what the next step is.

"Talon," Vicki says as I walk past.

I pause to look at her over my shoulder.

She offers me a genuine smile. "Thanks for taking care of my baby girl."

"You're welcome," I say sincerely. "I'll never not look out for Leni."

She regards me for a long moment before nodding.

Leni leads me to her front porch. When the door closes

behind us, she heaves out a sigh. "Well, that went about as well as I expected."

I snort. "You don't seem distraught over it though."

"Nah." She shrugs. "Dad will come around. He just processes things…slower than Mom."

I shake my head and wrap an arm around her waist. She rests her head on my shoulder.

"Can I take you to dinner tomorrow night, Leni?"

She gazes up at me. "I love how optimistic you are, Talon."

I peer down at her, frowning. "You didn't think I'd throw in the towel because your dad isn't thrilled for us, did you?"

"No." She presses a kiss to my chest, snuggling closer. "But he's going to go fucking brutal on you tomorrow. You'll be way too tired to go out to dinner." Her eyes meet mine, a playful spark of amusement in their depths. "I can come over and cook for you instead?"

I snort out a laugh even though her words ring true. Coach is going to put me through the grinder tomorrow. But knowing I can come home to a home-cooked meal and Leni? That alone makes it all worth it.

"I'll see you tomorrow night then."

"What would you like for dinner?"

"Surprise me."

She presses up on her tippy toes to brush a kiss over my lips. "I will."

"I'll leave a spare key for you at the front security desk. Come by whenever."

She nods. "Don't worry about Dad, Talon. This isn't easy for him, but his reaction has more to do with me and my dating a football player, then it does with you being upfront and honest. You're a good man and deep down, he knows I'd never do better than you."

I snort. "I'm not sure about that, Sunny Leni. Get a good night's sleep."

"I will. But only because I expect you to keep me up tomorrow night."

I laugh, shaking my head as I walk to my SUV. There's the confident, quirky woman from Coach's stories. I'm getting glimpses of sunshine again and even though my career, hell, my identity is on the line, it doesn't feel as terrifying as I thought.

Instead of overthinking how this decision will affect the team, I spend the night wondering what Leni is going to surprise me with for dinner tomorrow night.

19

Leni

"IT'S ABOUT TIME," MY SISTER ANSWERS THE PHONE THE following day.

I twirl a strand of hair around my finger and tug. "I'm sorry."

"Don't be sorry, Leni. Be real with me." Lincoln sounds hurt and that makes me feel worse.

But also, I know we'll be fine because we're sisters. We're ride or die for life.

"I miss you," I admit.

"I fucking miss you, too, you little shit." She goes off on me. But then, she snorts. "But I'm happy you called. What's been going on?" She gentles her tone.

"I had to leave Craig," I say slowly.

"No shit," she remarks. "How bad was it?"

"Bad."

Silence ticks by for a beat and I know Lincoln is wondering how hard to push me for information. "Are you ready to talk about it?"

"I'm getting there," I admit.

"Does Marlowe know?" my sister asks. My closeness with Marlowe never bothered Lincoln. She's always known our sister bond is strong, despite our close friendships or our ability to confide in others first. She always said as long as I had someone to talk to, she wouldn't press me too hard.

I clear my throat. "And Talon."

"Talon?" my sister asks. Then, she sucks in a breath, and I know it clicked. "The football player?"

I smile. "Yes."

"Mom didn't tell me that!"

"How often do you and Mom discuss me?"

"At least once a day," she says easily.

I snort. "She must have known I was getting ready to cave and call you."

"Probably," Lincoln agrees. "I've missed you, Leni. I want to hear everything about Talon. But...are you okay?"

"I'm getting there. So much has happened, Linc. And for so long, I was too embarrassed to admit it." I sigh. "How much time do you have?"

"For you? Eternity." Lincoln's tone is serious. Filled with compassion and understanding I don't deserve.

Crossing my legs, I lean back against the pillows on my bed and confide in my sister. I tell her about my final months in New York City, the fight with Craig that spurred me to call Mom, and coming home to Tennessee.

I share about the debutante ball organizing committee and Grandpa McIntyre. The things Marlowe is dealing with and trying to process. Dad pushing Talon into my life and appointing him my chaperone for a weekend.

"He didn't!" she gasps.

"He did."

Lincoln snorts. "And then it backfired."

I laugh with her. "Epically."

"Carry on," she says, more warmth in her tone now that we're past the part where I left Craig.

"We spent two nights together. At a quaint little inn by the lake. He took me to a water park. He saw the text messages from Craig and now, he knows everything. He even came clean with Dad."

"No," Lincoln breathes out. "Holy shit, Leni, that's *for real for real*."

"I know!" I exclaim. "He left a key for me at his place and I'm going over to cook him dinner tonight."

My sister's quiet for a beat before she says, "Are you sure that's a good idea, Len? You don't want to fall back into an old pattern, doing the same shit you tried with Craig."

I shake my head, even though she can't see me. "Trust me, I get where you're coming from. But this is nothing like that. He wanted to take me out to dinner, and I offered to come by so we can have a night in. Lincoln, Dad's going to demolish him today at practice."

"Oh, damn! I didn't even think of that. Do you think Dad will bench him?"

I drop my head back against the headboard. "I hope not."

"You definitely need to cook him dinner. Maybe even dessert."

I chuckle. "I've got plans for dessert," I say saucily.

"Oh my God! There's my sister. Welcome back to life, Leni. I've fucking missed you."

I laugh louder. "I've missed you too, Linc. When are you coming home for a visit?"

"Well, I haven't said anything to Mom or Dad yet but..."

"But?"

"I finished my master's degree."

"Yes, I know. We're all wondering what's next...?"

She laughs. "I accepted a job offer."

"In Germany?" I wonder.

"London!" my sister exclaims.

"Oh wow! That's amazing, Lincoln. Tell me about it."

As my sister begins to fill me in on her life—her interviewing process, her new job, the guy she had two dates with —I relax further. The pieces of my life are starting to fall back into place and I'm discovering my new normal.

It's even better than I thought.

When Lincoln and I hang up after an hour on the phone, I do so with a smile on my face.

Then, I spend a few hours working on debutante ball preparations since it's quickly approaching. I do some market research for the wedding planning company I'd like to launch. Eventually.

I check my phone, pleased that there are no new text messages from Craig. Did he finally get the message? Is he putting us in his rearview mirror the same way I have?

A little after lunchtime, I bound down the steps. I need to head to the grocery store so I can buy some ingredients for tonight's dinner—pasta alla Norma and a green salad.

"There you are!" Mom exclaims when she sees me. "What have you been up to today?"

"I talked to Linc."

Mom beams. "I love hearing that." She pulls some produce from the fridge and starts to chop vegetables. "We're having a stir-fry for dinner."

"Actually..." I bite my bottom lip and gesture toward the reusable canvas bags on the hook near the back door. "I'm cooking Talon dinner tonight."

"You are?" Mom's eyebrows rise. "What are you making?"

"Pasta alla Norma."

"A great choice," Mom says encouragingly.

"You're not upset?" I lean forward, propping my elbows on the kitchen island and snatching up a slice of red pepper.

"About you and Talon? No." Mom passes me another pepper slice and takes one for herself. She pauses in her chopping to regard me thoughtfully. "Leni, you came home a shell of yourself. The past few weeks, I've watched you find your way again. First, with the organizing committee. Then, with Marlowe. Now, with Talon. I know he has something bigger to do with you learning to trust yourself again. I also know there are things that you've chosen to keep to yourself about your relationship with Craig." She sighs and snaps her pepper slice in half, dropping both pieces onto the cutting board. "I hate watching you suffer, baby girl. And I am here for whatever you need. If you want to talk, I won't judge."

"I know, Mama."

"I'm just happy to see you happy again. And if that is because of Talon, how could I be upset? I'm grateful. I also know, from your dad and from my own interactions with him, that he's a really good guy. I've known that for a while. Dad does too; he'll come around."

"Eventually," I agree.

Mom smiles. "Need any help with your groceries?"

I tilt my chin toward the cutting board. "What about your stir-fry?"

She shrugs, pushing the cutting board farther onto the kitchen island. "It can wait. I'd rather be with you."

"I'd like that, too."

My mom reaches for her purse while I slip on some sandals and grab a few reusable bags. Then, we head out to her car, together, to go to the farmer's market and grocery store.

It's familiar and effortless. All the tension and fear I carried around my first few days at home has evaporated. Another missing piece snaps into place, and I feel an injection of lightness into my veins.

It's pure sunshine.

20
TALON

I can barely move when I let myself into my condo. My body is sore, and I'm exhausted after a grueling day of practice.

But the delicious scent of garlic and eggplant greets me and knowing that Leni is here eases some of my discomfort.

She comes out of the kitchen when she hears me. "How was it?" she asks, worrying her bottom lip between her teeth.

I hold my arms out to the sides, and she falls into them. "Nothing I can't handle," I assure her.

Just hugging her makes me feel better.

I tug on the end of her ponytail and her face meets mine. Grinning, I drop my mouth to hers to brush a kiss over her irresistible lips. "It smells good."

Leni blushes. "I hope you like dinner."

"I'm just happy to see you, Len."

She threads our fingers together to lead me toward the kitchen. I love having her here, seeing her in my space. She moves around the kitchen with ease, and I note the fresh flowers in a vase on the dining table. It makes me grin.

My space has been sparse for a long time. I never saw the point in decorating or getting a bunch of shit I don't need. In one day, Leni's managed to make it feel more like a home than a space I sleep at. And I like that too—it makes me wonder what it will look like, how it will feel, a few months from now.

"Was Dad awful?" She dishes some pasta into two bowls.

"No," I snort, shaking my head. I don't tell her that Coach definitely ramped up my conditioning. Or that my teammates noticed. I don't want to upset her or give her one more thing to worry about.

Instead, I want to enjoy dinner with her, curl up on the couch, and hold her close.

"Everything was fine. I just want to enjoy my time with you," I say, grabbing the salad bowl as we relocate to the dining table.

"Tell me about your day. What'd you do?" I ask once we're seated.

Leni beams. "I called my sister."

"You did? How is Lincoln?"

"She's great!" Leni proceeds to tell me about Lincoln, about grocery shopping with her mom, about Marlowe and the upcoming debutante ball.

I hang onto every word she shares. I love the details that color her stories—like the little boy who picked her a flower at the farmer's market. I love the way her eyes dance when she laughs—sky blue mixed with the Caribbean. I could sit and stare at her all day, feeling grateful to be swept up in her orbit.

Again, I understand what some of my teammates tried to tell me last season.

When you find the right woman, everything else pales in comparison. Even football.

After dinner, I wash the dishes. Leni argues with me, but I shake my head.

"You cooked, I clean," I remind her. Instead, I pour her a glass of wine and ask her to keep me company.

She does, sipping her wine slowly, while perched on the edge of the countertop, her legs swinging.

After I stow away the last pot, I step between her thighs and place my palms down on the outside of her hips. "I wish you could spend the night with me."

"Me too," she admits, placing down her wine glass and winding her arms around my neck. "I wish I could spend every night with you."

She kisses me softly and I grasp the backs of her thighs, lifting her easily. As Leni deepens our connection, I relocate us to my bedroom.

I lay her down in the center of my bed and stand to yank off my shirt. I toss it on the floor before dropping over Leni.

She wraps her arms around me again, pulling me closer until our lips meet. When her legs encircle my waist, I roll us over until my back meets the mattress and she straddles me.

I hold her hips, staring up at her. God, she's gorgeous.

The nervous anxiety she used to wear like a cloak has nearly disappeared. Instead, a confident, sexy version of her smirks at me, her blue eyes glowing. She plants her palms in the center of my chest before grinding against me slowly. Provocatively.

My cock stirs to life, needy as fuck for her heat. She continues to move her hips in slow, intoxicating circles.

I grip her hip, slipping one hand up her shirt. When my fingertips graze the edge of her bra, she begins to unbutton the row of buttons down the center of her shirt. She shimmies out of the shirt before reaching behind her to unhook her bra.

When that hits the floor, I moan, captivated by the way her tits bounce. I reach up to cup them, loving that they're the perfect handful for me.

Leni arches into my touch, slowing her pace until it's torturous.

"Fuck, baby," I murmur, my cock hard as a steel pipe. "You get me hard just by looking in my direction."

She smirks, her eyes clouding with lust. "No man's ever turned me on like you, Talon. I'm dripping for you."

"Fuck," I moan, loving that she wants me, hating the thought of her with any other man. *I'm her fucking man.*

I move to spin us again, to take control of this exchange, but Leni shakes her head. "Let me make this good for you, Talon."

"You make everything good for me," I say truthfully.

She nudges me back, pinning me down with her hands to my shoulders, before sliding down my body and dragging the waistband of my sweats with her. When my cock springs free, she laughs.

"No underwear?"

"Nope," I confirm.

"I like it," she says, her breath skating over the crown of my cock.

It fucking twitches and she grips me tighter. "Leni," I murmur.

"Let me, Talon," she says before her plump lips close over the head of my cock and I nearly fucking die.

I drop my head back, one hand moving to Leni's hair. My fingers tighten in her golden tresses, and I groan as she licks and sucks my shaft.

I've had blow jobs before. Plenty of fucking blow jobs. But knowing it's Leni—my fucking sunshine—bringing me pleasure, hits differently.

It's more than the physical act. It's sensual. Emotional. It's trusting.

She begins to work me over, her hand and mouth in tandem. Unable to stop myself, I begin to rock my hips, slowing fucking her gorgeous mouth.

At some point, her fingernails dig into my thigh, and I look up in concern. But in the next moment, her hand disappears and I hear her moan. The sound of wet arousal hits my eardrums, and I realize Leni is touching herself as she sucks my cock.

The realization, coupled with the visual, drives me higher and I swear, sitting up and rolling over her.

"I want to come inside of you, baby," I say, cupping her sex. "And if you're going to touch yourself, I want to watch." Taking her hand, I bring her fingers to her clit. "Show me," I mutter.

Leni holds my eyes, bold and so fucking sexy, as her fingers begins to rub her clit and two of mine enter her hot channel.

"Fuck, you're so fucking good," I sputter.

I watch her throat work a swallow. When her inner thighs begin to quake, I straddle her and replace my fingers with my cock.

Leni cries out in pleasure as I thrust into her slowly. Her fingers move rapidly over her clit, and I pick up the pace to match.

"I can't hold on," she admits.

"Then don't, baby. Let go. Come for me, Sunny."

She does. On a throaty cry, Leni orgasms. I get lost in her deep, blue eyes, rendered speechless by how damn gorgeous she looks coming on my cock. Two thrusts later and I follow her, spilling my want with her name on my lips.

Dropping forward, I roll us until we're lying side by side. She nuzzles me sweetly and I kiss the tip of her nose.

"I'm falling hard for you, Talon," she admits. "Make sure you catch me."

Again, I'm rendered speechless by her ability to make herself vulnerable. To share her truths honestly.

Noting the trust shimmering in her eyes, I decide to do the same. This woman has given me everything, the least I can do is be honest with her. I tuck a strand of her silky hair behind her ear and look right at her when I say, "I already fell, Leni. I'm waiting for you, baby. And I'll wait as long as you need."

She exhales slowly, her eyes filled with wonder. Then, she brushes her lips against mine. I kiss her back. Her palm drags up my side, and I begin to stiffen again, my cock already inside her.

She deepens our kiss and rocks her hips forward.

I groan and hold her face as I meet her, thrust for thrust.

We have sex again. Slow, deep, intense sex.

And somewhere between her release and mine, I comprehend that this is love.

I love Leni Strauss.

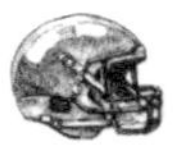

Things change after that. I'm so wrapped up in Leni, I don't protest the vigorous workouts Coach outlines for me. Or retort when he threatens to bench me before our season opener in front of the team. Or act hard when my teammates cast guarded, skeptical glances my way.

I ignore their taunts and ribbing. Bow out of drinks at Corks.

And try not to react when Coach Strauss openly ignores me, allowing Stevens to give me feedback instead of telling me things himself.

I continue to show up for practices and give one-hundred percent of myself to every workout, each training session. I hit the city pool, often with Leni in the next lane, to get those extra conditioning sessions in.

But each night, I come home to my girl. I get lost in her touch, her kiss, *her*.

And it feels like free-falling. Every day of my life feels like an unattainable high I never want to lose sight of.

"Miller!" Avery calls out.

I turn to glance over my shoulder. He jogs after me in the parking lot, catching me about two SUVs from mine.

"What's up?" I ask.

Avery sputters. "I should be asking you that."

I shrug.

"You're with Leni now, aren't you?"

"Yeah." My tone comes out harder than I intend.

"Take it easy." Avery laughs, holding up an open palm. "Look, for you to risk it all to be with her, I get that it's serious. The guys…" He tips his head toward the stadium. "They're just fucking with you."

"It's fine." I don't give a shit what anyone thinks anyway.

Avery shakes his head. "It's not. We miss you, man. Stop skipping out of practice as soon as you can. Come hang with us. Bring Leni along. If y'all are really making a go of this, you know we all have your back, right?"

I stall, shifting my weight from one foot to the next.

The truth is, I didn't know.

For the past few weeks, Coach has acted like I don't exist, and I assumed my teammates would take their lead from him.

"How serious is it?" Avery asks, his gaze curious.

"I love her," I admit.

I wait for him to swear. Instead, he grins. Clasps my shoulder. Gives it a little shake. "Then bring her for a fucking beer, man."

I frown. "You're serious?"

"Yeah," Avery says. "If she's your choice, celebrate it. Own it. Bring her around."

"But Coach—"

"You're a man, Miller. And Leni's an adult. Y'all are both capable of making your own decisions. And if Coach wanted to fuck over your career, he would have done so by now."

"He threatened to bench me," I remind him.

Avery shakes his head. "You're our only kicker. Coach was just pissed and running his mouth."

I sigh, knowing he's right. But Coach's outburst in front of the team still stings.

Avery smirks. "He's coming around, Talon. He just needs some time."

"Okay," I say slowly, still processing. "I'll bring Leni to Corks next time."

"After we win our next home game," Avery decides.

I snort. I like how he knows we'll win. Like it's a given. "Yeah, any time after her debutante ball on Friday. She's stressed about it and spending all her time at the country club."

"It's gonna be great," Avery says, waving a hand. "Those things follow a formula."

"You've been?"

He dips his head, looking embarrassed. "I'm from here, remember?"

"Right. Um, what am I supposed to wear?" I wait for Avery to laugh but he doesn't. He regards me for a second, understanding that this debutante ball is important to me because it's important to Leni.

He whistles low. "It's black tie, man. A black tuxedo, white shirt, black bow tie. See? A formula."

"Damn," I mutter. I didn't realize it was so…formal. "All right, thanks for the heads-up."

"It's a good time though. You'll have fun." Avery grins. "But not too much fun. We fly to Kansas City the day after."

"I won't be late."

"I know," he mutters. "I'm just giving you shit. Next week then? Corks?" He points at me for confirmation.

"We'll be there."

21

Leni

"Missed you," I say the moment Talon walks through the door to his condo.

He grins and holds his arms open. "This is a nice surprise."

"I'm glad I caught you." I step into his embrace and kiss him hello.

His forehead wrinkles. "Today is…tea?"

"That was yesterday. Today is a luncheon."

"And tomorrow is the big night."

"Yes!" I snuggle deeper into his arms. "I'm really excited for this event. I just hope it all goes smoothly."

"It's going to be great." Talon releases me and takes my hand to pull me deeper into his living room. "Sit with me for a minute. Catch me up."

We lean back on the couch, turning toward each other. Between the start of football season and the approaching deb ball, I've barely seen him. We steal moments whenever we can and try to eat dinner together at least one night a week, but it's been tough.

I may be on cloud nine in my personal life, but living under Dad's roof hasn't been a picnic. He oscillates between ignoring me and trying to pick a fight with me by making condescending, Talon-related comments.

At least, he was. Over the past few days, it seems like he's starting to come around.

Raia told me that Dad threatened to freaking bench Talon for the first game, which was insane—the Coyotes don't have another kicker.

The fact that Talon didn't blink twice aggravated my father further, which Mom found amusing.

However, as the debutante ball approaches and Dad sees how supportive and helpful Talon's been, his coldness toward Talon is beginning to thaw.

He asked me twice if Talon is attending the ball on Friday night. He even grunted, begrudgingly and with a modicum of respect, after the second time I confirmed Talon's attendance.

That, coupled with the way Mom's been singing Talon's praises—he helped her garden last week—is forcing Dad to realize that Talon and me being together is for real.

This isn't a rebellious phase on my part, and this isn't Talon trying to pull one over on the Coach either.

"The events this week have been good. Adeline's been enjoying everything. I don't know what is going on with Marlowe's family; to be honest, I don't think she does either. But her mom didn't show up to the Mother-Daughter tea yesterday."

"Shit," Talon whispers, his eyes widening.

"Adi was okay," I rush to explain, placing a hand on his forearm. "Marlowe came instead."

"That's good." Talon pulls me into his lap. "I missed you."

"Me too." I snuggle deeper. "Great game in Buffalo."

I feel the curve of his smile against the back of my neck. "You tuned in?"

"I watch all the games." I point to myself. "Coach's daughter."

Talon snorts. "Don't remind me."

I turn in his arms, straddle him, and kiss him hard.

"How much time do we have?" he asks, sliding his fingers though my hair and holding the back of my neck.

"Just enough," I assure him, pressing my mouth back to his.

"Do you want to see my tuxedo first?" he asks, grinding against me.

"You got one?" I ask, surprised by his thoughtfulness. While there is a formal dress code, I didn't want to pressure Talon into obtaining a tuxedo and make him feel uncomfortable.

"Wait 'til you see me in it…" He trails kisses down my neck.

"I want to see." I push against him gently, not wanting to end this moment but also curious to see him in his tuxedo.

He chuckles, drawing up the hem of my shirt. "I'll surprise you, baby," he replies, his eyes flashing. Then, he wastes no time, turning us so I'm lying on my back and he's hovering over me. His eyes hold mine—deep and brimming with sincerity—and my heart beats a little faster.

"What is it?" I wonder.

He shakes his head once, a small smile playing over his lips. "I love you, Leni Strauss." He admits it on an exhale before dipping his head and kissing me softly. "I love you so damn much."

I draw in a sharp breath, my mind spinning. Wrapping my legs around Talon's waist, I tug him closer. He falls on top of me and we both laugh.

I grasp his face between my hands and stare back at him. "Good. Because I love you, too." Then, I kiss him hard.

And we make the most of the rest of our time together.

We come together eagerly. It's intense and emotional. We give each other our hearts along with our bodies.

And even cloud nine can't hold me back. With Talon's words echoing in my mind, his kiss on my lips, and his love wrapping around me like a shield, I float even higher.

"She looks gorgeous," I breathe out to Marlowe as Adi is announced.

The venue is perfect. The tables are evenly spaced around the dance floor with gold Chiavari chairs, flickering candles, and beautiful cream and peach peony floral arrangements. The setting is sun-kissed Tennessee at its finest and I love that I had the opportunity to be part of this day.

To witness Adeline, a girl I've known since her birth, the younger sister I never had, descend the stairs and meet her escort, the son of a family friend, brings a smile to my face.

"Her dress is gorgeous," I murmur, admiring the white, A-line gown that fits Adi like a glove.

"Aunt Rose Marie bought it for her," Marlowe explains.

I nod, realizing that Marlowe's family issues are deeper than I understand. The fact that Marlowe's parents would bail on this event—on something that is important to Adeline—highlights how low the McIntyre family has sunk.

I haven't pressed Marlowe for information, but I hope she knows that she has me—and Keller and his family—to soften the hits that keep coming.

"Talon cleans up well," Marlowe murmurs, lifting her chin to the side of the ballroom where Talon and Keller are standing.

Keller swirls his glass of red wine while Talon sips on a sparkling water. Regular season has started, and he's boarding a plane to Kansas City tomorrow. The fact that he's here tonight… well, even Dad can't refute the fact that Talon is as invested in this relationship as I am. Especially since Dad had to bow out of attending tonight's ball when a last-minute meeting came up.

I don't blink as I check Talon out. Damn, does he wear a tuxedo well. One would never know he's only dressed up a handful of times in his life. He rocks the look effortlessly—pure swagger. Plus, that bow tie is a classical touch that I can't stop admiring.

When he notes my eyes on him, he lifts his drink in my direction and gives me a wink. I bite my bottom lip to keep from blowing him a kiss.

I love you, Leni. I love you so damn much.

It means a lot to me that Talon is here to support me. Celebrating this achievement with me, he's fully invested in my success. I can't wait to dance with him later.

I return my gaze to the top of the stairs as the next debutante is presented.

Jasmine begins her descent. Beside me, Marlowe shifts. Her hand wraps around my wrist and squeezes.

I glance at her. "What—"

"Leni," my best friend whispers, shock and concern blooming in her expression.

I follow her line of sight and feel like the floor bottoms out beneath me.

Craig is standing at the bar, casually holding a glass of scotch, and staring right at me. His eyes are piercing—dark and angry. His expression is carefully neutral, barely concealing the fury I know lurks beneath. His eyes cut to Talon before slamming back to mine. Betrayal washes across his expression, before morphing into anger.

He is livid. And he is here to make a scene.

My blood runs cold and the back of my neck prickles. My fight-or-flight response activates and I hate that the first thing I do is check for the exits.

My pulse skitters, my stomach twists in dread, and the taste of fear floods my mouth.

Craig smirks, knowing I'm scared. Liking that I'm scared. That I'm considering running.

Marlowe swears, garnering a look of disgust from a

nearby guest. I'm too rattled to reprimand her. Her hand settles on my back, and I draw strength from her proximity.

Then, my gaze swings to Talon and he's frowning at me, knowing that something is wrong. Fully aware that I'm about to spiral.

Shit, I need to get out of here. I need to diffuse the situation.

The next debutante is presented.

Craig places his scotch down and takes a menacing step in my direction.

How did I not see this coming? The only reason I didn't block Craig weeks ago is so I would have a pulse on his mindset and yet…he's managed to catch me off guard.

Oh, God, he's going to cause a scene. He's going to ruin this event and everything I worked for. He's going to rattle my confidence and topple the life I've rebuilt this summer.

Talon's neck snaps in Craig's direction and he hands Keller his glass.

Surprise and confusion blanket Keller's expression as Marlowe curls her body toward mine.

"We should move," she says, keeping her voice low. Her arm links with mine and she grasps my hand. "We should—"

"I've been looking everywhere for you, Leni," Craig's voice rings out. It's loud and booming and causes nearby tables to turn in our direction.

Annoyance flickers through the crowd, frustrated by Craig's interruption and blatant disregard for the presentations taking place. He always was a cocky bastard, putting himself before everything. Even decades of tradition.

"You didn't come home, sweetheart," he continues, reaching for my other wrist and tugging harshly. Marlowe's fingers dig in and for a second, I feel like the middle of a tug-of-war. "And now I find you here, smiling so prettily for—"

"Get your fucking hand off her." Talon's voice is low but edged in steel. It's frigidly cold, and shivers run up my spine.

He's glaring at Craig with a look I've never seen him wear before. It's furious, calculated, and downright dangerous.

Craig chuckles, shrugging nonchalantly.

"Holy shit, he's fucking deranged," Marlowe murmurs, still plastered against my side.

Craig wraps his arm around me and grabs my ass. I flinch but don't shake him off. I don't move. I can't. I'm frozen.

It's as if I've vacated my body and am watching the scene unfold as a neutral, third-party bystander.

"Well, I never," a nearby guest gasps, literally clutching her pearls.

If I wasn't fighting off the cold numbness spreading through my limbs, I would laugh at how cliché it is. But I can't laugh, or speak, or even move.

Talon doesn't miss a beat. His arm darts out and smacks Craig's hand away. Craig's palm slips off my ass and Marlowe pulls me back a step.

Craig turns toward Talon, squaring up and grinning. He's taunting him and before I can clue Talon in, Talon takes the bait and snaps. He catches Craig with a clean jab across the face before closing his hand around Craig's throat.

Phantom pain blossoms along my collarbone but the longer I stare at Talon and Craig, the more it fades, until a healing touch—with the lightness of a feather—grazes along my throat in its wake.

Marlowe sucks in a breath. Keller's face looms nearby. Silence pierces the ballroom—thunderingly loud to negate the complete quiet.

"You'll never put another hand on her again," Talon continues, unbothered by the hundred pairs of eyes gawking at him in horror. "I'll fucking kill you before that happens."

The scary thing is, he means it.

As Craig's face turns red and he begins to sputter for air, some part of my mind wonders if he's going to end him right here.

"Talon, ease up," Keller warns.

That night at Toby's lake house rolls though my mind. Talon with his hand around Toby's neck. Keller trying to ease the tension.

Déjà vu hits me square in the face and the only thing I'm capable of doing is blinking. I blink.

Craig swats at Talon's arm. Once. Twice.

And then, something breaks.

Nearby guests are on their feet. Men rush Talon, tackling him from behind. Still, he goes down swinging, managing to catch Craig across the face for a second time and once in the stomach.

I watch as Craig's head snaps back. Blood flies from his nose and lip in slow motion, splattering a nearby debutante's pristine white gown.

That stain will never come out.

I shake my head at my thought. But still, I don't move. I can't.

"Breathe." Marlowe shakes my shoulder.

At her command, I suck in a gulp of oxygen.

"She's in shock," Marylee declares.

And then, Mom's at my side. Her arm is around my waist, ushering me to the side of the room. Away from Talon.

Where's Talon?

I crane my neck, trying to spot him.

"You don't have to see this," Marylee says.

But I do. I need him. He's protecting me. He's keeping me safe.

Talon's pressed against the floor, the knee of a police officer digging into his back as he's handcuffed.

He doesn't resist arrest. He doesn't say a word. Instead, his eyes find mine and I read the concern in his dark eyes.

He's worried…for me.

Beside him, a paramedic checks out Craig. Oh no! They're worrying about the wrong guy.

I open my mouth to scream but no sound comes out.

Instead, a small smirk turns the corners of Craig's lips as he glances at me. *See you soon*, he mouths.

A shudder runs through me, locking down my limbs. I nearly collapse as my knees buckle.

"I got her." Keller scoops me up and carries me from the room.

"She needs water." Mom hurries beside us.

I'm taken to a private seating area in the venue. The floral arrangements in the space are the same as the centerpieces on the tables in the ballroom and it strikes me as odd how delicate they look. Sweet and pretty and fragile.

A blanket is wrapped around my shoulders. A water bottle and a teacup are set down on the table in front of me. Mom and Marlowe sit on the sofa on either side of me, bracketing me like book ends. Keller paces in front of the room, guarding the door like a caged lion. Time passes both quickly and slowly. In fact, I lose sense of it altogether as a heaviness cloaks the room and presses down on me.

"Adeline is with Jasmine's family," Keller tells Marlowe who lets out a sigh of relief.

"Leni, Leni, why didn't you tell me?" Mom sobs into her hands. "Has he hurt you? Threatened you?"

I work a swallow. My throat is so dry, it feels cracked. But I need to come clean. I need to admit everything to Mom. I've waited too damn long.

"Why didn't I see the signs?" Mom continues, blaming herself.

It's not your fault! The thought yells in my mind but I can't make myself say the words.

"Leni," Mom says, staring straight at me. "How long has Talon been hurting you?"

Wait.

What?

I gape at Mom. Sound comes rushing back, exploding in

my eardrums like bombs. I shake from the accusation, my fingers trembling as they bunch the fabric of my gown.

"It's okay. You don't have to be afraid. I'm here," Mom continues, reaching for my trembling, unsteady hands.

I close my eyes as another shudder wracks through my body.

They have the wrong man.

"Mom," I whimper, trying to clear my throat.

"Where is she?" Dad growls, bursting into the room and pushing past Keller. "I got here as fast as I could."

Marlowe jumps to her feet, leaving the space next to me vacant for Dad. She joins her cousin by the door and the two of them try to give us as much privacy as possible while ensuring random people don't enter.

"What the fuck happened, Leni?" Dad's voice booms.

"Shh! Don't yell at her!" Mom shouts.

Regret washes over Dad's face as he yanks at his hair, clearly at a loss over what to do.

He strides back and forth in front of the coffee table for a few beats, similar to Keller a few minutes ago.

"It's Craig," I admit on a whisper.

Dad stops and glares at me. Mom stiffens beside me. Marlowe breathes a sigh of relief.

"What's Craig?" Dad asks. "I spoke to the Chief of Police. Craig's okay, by the way. Talon could have really—"

"Craig hit me," I cut him off, needing him to know the truth. "Threatened me. Hurt me." My voice grows stronger with each admission.

I look up and meet Dad's bewildered expression.

"I didn't know how to tell you. But for weeks, months, Craig controlled me. Threw a bottle of scotch against the wall in a fit of rage. Choked me." I reach for my collarbone. "That's why I left New York." I look at Mom, tears welling in my eyes. "That's why I came home."

"Oh, Leni." Mom wraps an arm around my shoulders,

pulling me closer. "Oh, God. You're okay, sweet girl. Everything's okay."

"He's been sending me text messages since I came home. I was too scared to block him. And I felt safe here because of Dad and-and Talon." My voice breaks on his name. "I thought Craig's messages would give me insight into his thoughts. A warning if he ever came to Knoxville. But...he showed up."

Mom hugs me harder as I sob. The numbness is thawing, and my cries come out in large, loud gasps. Mom holds me as I fall apart, and it feels infinitely easier knowing I can rely on her to piece me back together.

When my wails subside into whimpers, I chance a look at Dad.

He looks like someone just tore his heart out. His eyes bleed with regret, his mouth twisted in shame.

"He put his hands on you," he murmurs.

I nod.

"That's why Talon..."

"Yeah," I confirm. "Talon knows. Everything," I add, hating the betrayal that sparks in my dad's eyes at my admission that I confided in my new boyfriend before him.

"Are you okay?" he asks instead.

Mom's arms tighten around me.

"I will be," I manage to say truthfully. I blink back some tears.

Dad swears and straightens, brushing a hand over his head. He looks at Keller. "Can you get my girls home safely?"

"Of course," Keller says.

"Where are you going?" Mom asks.

"Daddy, where's Talon?" I wonder.

Dad shakes his head, looking miserable. "Talon's in jail. And Craig is roaming fucking free." His jaw tics. "But not for long." He points at Mom and me. "I'll see you at home."

Mom nods. I cry at the thought of Talon being locked up in a jail cell.

As I drop my head to Mom's shoulder and bury my face, the door slams closed.

"Freddy's going to fix everything," Marlowe declares.

And God, I hope she's right.

But deep down, I don't know if this can be fixed.

My inability to take Craig's messages seriously, my inaction in filing a police report or even telling my parents, created this disaster.

I ruined the debutante ball.

I got Talon arrested.

And now—will the team drop him?

Have I ruined his career? Have I ruined us?

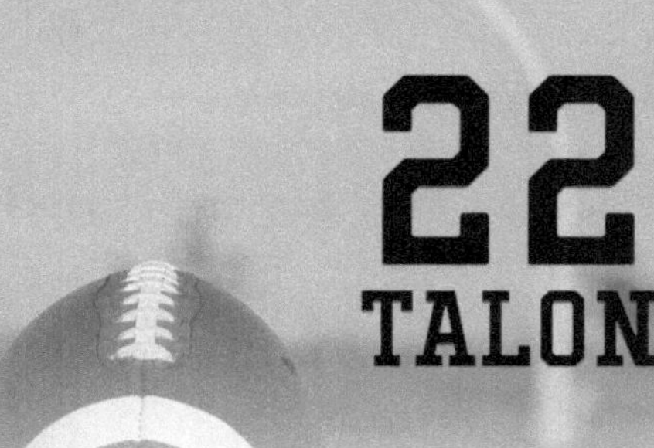

22
TALON

The worst thing about being behind bars is worrying about Leni.

I fucking hate that I'm here, spinning every horror story imaginable, while that fuckwad Craig is walking around with access to my girl.

My beautiful ray of sunshine who was too panicked to speak. Or move. Or even breathe.

Noting the way Leni shut down wrecked me. A shot of adrenaline burned through my veins, and the second I saw Craig touch her, I was moving. At that moment, I didn't give a fuck who was watching, or recording, me. I didn't care about anything other than making sure Craig didn't hurt Leni.

And then, he fucking groped her ass. Touched her without her permission. Scared her. Again.

I lost it and the only thing I regret is that I'm stuck here, in a damn jail cell, and Leni's out there with no way to contact me.

"Miller. You got a visitor," an officer calls out.

I sit up straighter but don't bother responding.

Before I can decide on who I think it is—my bets are between Keller and Avery—Coach appears on the other side of the cell.

"Coach." I jump to my feet.

Coach stares at me. He widens his stance and crosses his arms over his chest.

Shit. *Is Leni okay? Did something else happen?*

I let out a nervous exhale.

On a logical level, I know my entire career is in a precarious position. There's video footage of me choking Craig and threatening his life. There is an entire room of witnesses to craft their own versions of what happened.

My career and everything I worked for, hustled toward, is on the line.

And the only person I care about is Leni.

"Is she okay?" I ask.

At my question, Coach sighs heavily. His shoulders slump and his head drops. The weight of the world has rested on his shoulders for so long and now, he's buckling beneath it.

"You knew?" he tosses back.

About Craig. He must mean about Craig.

But I'm not blowing up Leni's spot or sharing anything that she hasn't told her parents. I won't do that to her.

"How is she?" I ask again.

Coach's head snaps up, his eyes flashing. He doesn't like me asking questions, but I don't care. I'm too twisted up over Leni and her safety to give a shit about anything else, even Coach Strauss's opinion of me.

"She told us the truth," Coach says, wrapping a hand around one of the bars.

I breathe out. Thank God. "And Craig?"

"I took care of him." There's a sharpness to Coach's tone and I narrow my eyes, trying to understand why he seems angry with me.

But then, I get it. I'm the guy his daughter came to instead of him.

And he's a dad, worried out of his mind, and not fully ready to step aside and cede a position he's carried for so long to another guy in Leni's life.

"Good," I say, and I mean it. I'll protect Leni with everything I have but at the end of the day, I want her safe. It doesn't matter to me who makes it happen as long as it's done.

"She told you first." Coach sounds accusatory.

"She didn't want to disappoint you."

"Fuck." He shakes his head. "Fuck, Miller. I should've known."

"Yeah," I agree. "But she was dealing with a lot…and to be fair, Coach, I guessed at it."

"Guessed?" Surprise flickers in his eyes.

"That night at the lake house, the shit that went down with Toby, I saw Leni's reaction. And it reminded me of my mom." I shrug, hating that I was right about it. "There were other things too but don't beat yourself up over it. Sometimes, it takes an outside perspective, some distance, to see things for what they are. You two are close, you always were."

Coach's jaw clenches, anger, hurt, and relief all warring for position in his expression. "Thank you, Talon. For being there for her."

"I'll always step up for her. I'm not going anywhere, Coach. I know you never wanted Leni with a football player, and trust me, I know there are better men for her than me. But I love her. She's it for me. And if you need to take your anger out on me for the rest of the season to prove some point, or put me in the place you want me, go ahead. I'm not walking away from her. Not for fucking anything, not even for you. Not even for football."

Coach stares at me hard. Seconds pass and I hold his gaze, neither of us blinking. Then, he nods. "You'll be out within the hour."

"Coach?"

He sighs, looking tired. "The Attorney General is a huge Coyotes fan. I made a few calls, and you'll get slapped with some community service."

Holy shit. I hang my head as waves of relief, of gratitude, roll through me. "Thank you, Coach." I meet his eyes. "Fuck. Thank you."

He nods once.

"I'll see you at the airport tomorrow."

He shakes his head. "Nah, come by the house once you're out."

"I will. I'll be there."

Coach continues to stare at me.

"What?" I ask, growing uncomfortable.

"You earned your spot on the field, Miller. You're one hell of a kicker and an asset to the team. My issue with you and Leni is just that—*mine*. I didn't like that I didn't see your relationship coming, but that's on me. You earned your place by Leni's side. You stood up for her when she needed you. You're one hell of a man, Talon. You're good enough for my daughter. But you don't need me to tell you that. You need to believe it and know, deep down, that what you two share is special. It's enough."

He turns to leave, and I reach out. "Wait."

Coach stops and lifts an eyebrow. "Thank you," I say, meaning it. "If I hadn't met you, if you hadn't helped me, I don't think Leni ever would have looked at me twice."

Coach holds my gaze, and I see the moment he gets it, truly understands that his daughter chose me, in part, because of him. He snorts softly and shakes his head. "The world works in mysterious ways, Miller. See you tonight." He glances at his watch. "Hopefully before midnight."

"See you, Coach."

"Make sure your head's screwed on right for Sunday's game," he adds as he walks away. He turns around again before he exits the space. "Don't worry about that son of a bitch from New York either. There won't be another problem."

"Got it," I say, knowing Craig's been handled. Will I ever

know the full extent of what that means? Probably not. But I'm cut from a similar cloth as Coach Strauss, so I trust that when he says I don't need to worry, I don't need to give it a second thought.

I plop back down in the cell and wait to be released. I'm sprung within the hour, with community service hours like Coach said. My agent, Callie, is already on the line to discuss a PR recovery strategy.

"Callie, can I call you tomorrow?" I ask as I duck into the car waiting out front to take me to the Strauss residence.

"Sure," Callie says. "But call me first thing, Talon. We need to get ahead of the narrative on this. I need to know, as soon as possible, how you want to spin it."

"I'll get back to you," I say, knowing a lot of that will depend on what Leni is comfortable sharing. I'm not going to push her to share her story or paint Craig a certain way. If she never wants to spill a detail of her past with him, then I'll publicly take the heat and move on.

"You got lucky today, Talon," Callie says quietly.

As the houses outside the window blur together and the car I'm in approaches Coach's house, I spot Leni sitting on the front porch, waiting for me.

I grin as soon as I see her. "Don't I know it," I mutter, ending the call.

When the car pulls into the driveway, Leni is bounding down the stairs to meet me. As soon as I step out, she lunges into my waiting arms.

I catch her easily, one arm supporting her legs, the other cradling the back of her neck. I kiss her hard and she hugs me tightly.

"Thank God you're okay," I breathe, resting my forehead against hers.

"I'm so glad you're out," she replies, peppering my cheeks, my nose, my eyelids with kisses. "Thank you for today, Talon. I'm so sorry I—"

"You have nothing to apologize for."

"I do." She pulls back, disappointment lining her expression. "I should have done a lot of things differently. I wish I had spoken up weeks ago about Craig. Now it's a 'he said, she said' situation and…" She trails off. "You got stuck in the middle."

I place her on her feet, shaking my head. "Baby, don't you get it? As long as you're safe and happy, I don't care."

"Well, I do." She takes my hand and pulls me toward the house.

The car that dropped me off backs out of the driveway.

"I begged Dad to connect me to your agent," Leni continues.

"Callie? We just hung up." I look at Leni expectantly.

She blushes. "I know. She said I had to talk to you but Talon, I'm ready to go public. My dad's from New York, you know?"

"Yeah," I say. His family immigrated to a small, cottage town, Honey Harbor.

"He's calling in every marker he has—to the DA in New York, who he knows from undergrad. To the AG here in Tennessee—"

"Who's apparently a fan," I murmur.

"Yeah." She nods. "There was another woman who filed a police report against Craig years ago. The District Attorney in New York is going to investigate it. I've filed a restraining order against Craig in the meantime." Leni lowers her gaze. "I spoke with my parents." She pulls in a breath. "I'm thinking about pressing charges."

"You are?" My eyes widen. "I'm so proud of you, baby."

"But what if he comes after you in retaliation?" she says, looking worried.

"Leni…" I shake my head. "No way. If you want to press charges—"

"I want to tell the world what he did to me, Talon. I want

everyone to know that you were protecting me. I want to help save your reputation the way you've saved me. And I want us to move past this, together."

I stop walking and wait until she turns toward me. Then, I wrap my arms around her and kiss her hard. "I want everything with you, Sunny. I'll play this any way you want, as long as it's what you want."

"Good." She grins, looking more confident and at ease than she should after such a stressful day. "Then leave it to me."

I bend down to kiss her. My hand fists in her hair and I barely feel the sting from hitting Craig only a handful of hours ago.

The porch lights flicker on and off and Leni and I jump apart.

Vicki stands in the doorway laughing. "I haven't had to do that in long time."

I look at Leni, raising an eyebrow.

She shrugs. "It wasn't for me."

"It was for Lincoln," Vicki explains, holding the door open for us.

When I step over the threshold, Vicki hugs me. "Thank you for everything you've done for our daughter."

"It was nothing," I say, unsure how to handle these emotions. The Strauss women have no problem embracing vulnerability.

Vicki shakes her head. "It was important, Talon. The way you protected her, the way she confided in you, it matters. Come on." She loops her arm through mine and leads me into the dining room where Coach and Leni are already seated. "I hope you like pizza."

Various pizzas are spread out down the center of the table along with a green salad and a Caprese salad.

"This beats debutante ball dinner any day," I joke.

Coach laughs, Leni rolls her eyes, and Vicki grins.

I sit down at the dining table. All eyes turn to Coach, who lifts his beer in the air. "To Talon," he says, causing a lump to swell in my throat. "Welcome to the family, son."

Tears spring to Leni's eyes. She reaches for my hand beneath the table, and I lace our fingers together.

For the first time, I feel like I belong to something other than a football team. I belong to Leni and the Strauss family.

It's a homecoming I never knew I needed but, in this moment, it feels like winning the Super Bowl.

"Thank you, Coach."

He nods. "If you think this means I'm gonna go easy on you…" He lets his sentence hang in the air. "I'm not."

Leni laughs while Vicki smiles at her husband.

"I'd expect nothing less," I say, meaning it.

Coach holds his own to a higher standard and I'm honored to be included among them.

"Come on, come on." I bounce on my toes, clasping Lincoln's hand.

"He's gonna make the extra point," Marlowe says breezily from my other side.

Lincoln grins and hugs me closer.

She surprised us with a visit before she relocates to London, and I couldn't be happier to have her home.

Or to have her sit beside me and cheer for Talon and the Coyotes in tonight's game against New Jersey. Right now, it feels like old times, and I'm savoring the feeling. Nostalgia intertwines with anticipation over the next play and I'm nearly giddy as Talon walks onto the field.

He's pure swagger, looking undeniably sexy in his football uniform.

He glances up to the stands where he knows I'm sitting. I can't see his eyes or read his lips, but I know he's looking right at me when he lifts a hand in the air.

"Damn," Lincoln murmurs, clutching my fingers.

"Here we go, baby," I whisper.

I hold my breath as the snap takes place. I zero in on Talon as he dances a few steps forward and swings his leg, kicking the ball in a perfect arc. He scores the extra point, giving the Coyotes a one-point lead, and the entire stadium erupts.

There are roars of jubilation. There's dancing and tipped

beers. There's a wave of excitement that sweeps me up in its current, and I laugh out loud, loving the thrill of this moment.

Loving that I'm here to support my guy. To finally show up for him.

The clock runs out a few minutes later and the Coyotes secure another win.

"Hell yeah!" Linc cheers, pulling me into a hug.

"That was one hell of a game," Marlowe agrees, clinging to my other arm.

I smile at my sister and best friend. "Are y'all ready to head to Corks?" I ask. I promised Talon I would come hang out with the team after the game. It surprised me that Avery asked him when he would bring me around, but I suppose being the coach's daughter and being Talon's girlfriend are two different things.

As much as I relished the title of the first, I am in love with the position of the second. I adore being Talon's girlfriend. It happened quicker than I could have imagined but every step along the way felt right.

Real.

For the hopeless romantic who nearly gave up hope, I feel stronger than ever. Talon helped me find my confidence again and know that I'm capable of making my own choices. Of trusting my gut. Of believing in the more.

I am worthy. I am enough.

And together, we're everything I've ever hoped for.

"I'm going to bow out," Marlowe says, surprising me.

Lincoln frowns. "You sure?"

"Yeah," Marlowe says, nodding. "I've got some family stuff to sort through."

I give my friend a hug. "Call me if you need anything."

"I will," she whispers. It's been a tough few weeks for Marlowe and her family. I don't know all the ins and outs, but I know a lot of change is occurring in the McIntyre household. While Marlowe is doing everything she can to shield

Adi from the brunt of it, I'm doing whatever I can to make sure she knows she has a support system too.

Marlowe gives us a wave as she gestures toward the exit.

"Let's give the crowd a few minutes to thin out," Lincoln suggests.

I agree and sit back down. My sister and I sit in comfortable silence, staring at the field, which was like a second home to us growing up.

"Can you believe I moved back home?" I ask, nudging her with my shoulder.

Lincoln laughs. "Yeah," she says, staring at me. "You fit in it here, Leni. Seeing you with Talon… This is the right place for you. But I don't know if you would have realized that without giving New York City a fair chance. I'm glad you had that experience, even though I hate what happened with Craig."

"Me too," I murmur. "But you're right. If I hadn't gone to New York, I may have wondered—what if? Now, I just want to be wherever Talon is."

Lincoln smiles. "I'm happy for you, Leni Lou." She gestures toward the exit. We stand and she loops her arm with mine as we make our way out of the stands. "I haven't been to Corks in ages."

"Me neither." I laugh. "I can't believe you're only in town for a few days. I wish you could stay longer."

"Me too. I've missed you." Lincoln drops her head to mine. She hugs me closer. "Tell me, for real, how are you holding up?" she asks, her blue eyes, the same shade as mine, studying me.

"I'm…doing okay," I admit. "I was scared to press charges, but once they were filed, I felt so much better. I started seeing a therapist last week and I think that's going to be helpful."

"I saw your social media posts. I'm proud of you for

blasting the hell out of that dickwad." A small smirk touches my sister's lips.

"Yeah," I agree, nodding. "I put a lot of thought into what I wanted to say. But I never expected that post to go viral."

"Did he really lose his job?" Lincoln wonders.

I nod. "Did Mom tell you what else happened?"

"No! What?"

"Another ex-girlfriend of his, Lisa, reached out. The same thing had happened to her, and she felt powerless about it. She wasn't sure what to do or who to confide in. But now that he's been put on blast, she came forward and is pressing charges as well."

"Shut up!" my sister exclaims.

I shake my head. "I don't know if they'll stick."

"Did you feel better, after pressing charges, and talking to Lisa?"

"I did. Every day gets a little bit easier. Talon's been my rock through it all. I wouldn't have made it this far without him, Linc."

"I had no idea how bad it was, Len."

"You weren't supposed to. I didn't want you to."

"I'm sorry," she says as we near the entrance to the locker rooms.

"I'm sorry, too. No more secrets, okay?"

"Promise me?" Lincoln holds out her pinky, the way she did when we were kids.

I snort and pinky promise her. "Swear it."

"The Strauss sisters back in action," the security guard, Priest, calls out as we near the door.

"Here we are, Priest!" I grin, my arm still looped with my sister's.

"Troublemakers." He snorts, before looking at Lincoln. "Good to see you, Linc."

Lincoln blushes slightly and I roll my lips together to keep from laughing. She's had a crush on Priest for years.

"You too, Priest," she manages as he waves us through the door.

When it closes behind us, we erupt in giggles, the same way we did in high school. A few people in the hallways grin at our reaction, and a few give us strange looks, which only makes us laugh harder.

"Hey! What's so funny?" Dad asks as he walks toward us.

We shake our heads in unison, sputtering to come up with words that will make sense.

Dad grins and wraps his arms around us, kissing the tops of our heads. "Missed you, girls."

"Missed you, too, Dad," Lincoln says.

I snuggle closer and inhale.

Everything in my world feels right again. Real.

"Great game, Miller," someone says, and I break away from Dad. My eyes dart behind him to find Talon.

Dad smacks a hand over his heart as if I've wounded him, and Lincoln snickers.

"She's all grown up now, Daddy," Lincoln jokes.

"Never," Dad growls.

In the next moment, I'm swept clear off my feet as Talon lifts me up.

"Great game, baby!" I say, kissing him hard.

"I can't watch," Dad groans good-naturedly, turning away.

"I can," Lincoln replies.

Talon laughs and hugs me for a moment before placing me on my feet. "Glad you could make the game, Lincoln. I know you're only here for a few days."

"As if this one would let me skip it." Lincoln juts her thumb toward Dad as Talon hugs her hello.

"Welcome home, Linc!" Cohen says, passing by. He points at us. "You coming to Corks?"

"As long as Raia will be there," Lincoln replies.

Cohen grins. "She wouldn't miss it."

"See you there," I say as Talon slips an arm over my shoulders.

"I'll get both your girls home safely, Coach," he tells Dad who rolls his eyes.

Then, we leave the stadium behind, pile into Talon's SUV, and head to Corks to celebrate another Coyotes win.

"I love that you're dating Talon!" Raia Callaway says, hugging me hello.

"I love that you're playing professional soccer," I shoot back, smiling at her teammate who is in town with her this weekend. While I've seen Raia a few times at games, I haven't had many chances to catch up with her this season. She splits her time between Knoxville and Chicago, where she plays for the Chicago Tornadoes.

"Me too." Raia grins, her eyes dancing. "And you're back home too, Linc!"

"Just for a few days," Lincoln says. "Then, I'm off to London."

"London!" Raia exclaims. "We need drinks. I want to know everything." She clasps Lincoln's arm and tugs her toward the bar where her teammate is ordering another round.

While they raise their glasses in a toast, I'm pulled into a conversation with Jag. Then, I stop to chat with Kiki, one of the sports reporters who regularly covers the Coyotes.

"Len! Drink!" My sister holds a margarita in the air for me.

"Better go get that," Kiki says.

I say goodbye to her and make my way to Lincoln. "Thanks." I take the glass from her hand.

She clinks her margarita against mine. "It's like old times, yeah?"

"Yeah," Avery says, coming up behind us. "Except Leni is dating Talon so I'm not worried about Coach flipping out that one of his players flirted with his daughter."

Talon laughs. "Yep. That ship has sailed."

"Not yet for me," my sister shares, raising a palm. "Still single."

"There's no rush, Linc," Cohen offers, stepping into our huddle.

"Hey, guys," West Crawford announces, popping his head into the mix. "I gotta take off."

"Baby duty?" Cohen jokes.

West grins. "I miss my girls. Don't hate."

"Never," Talon says, smirking. But his tone conveys his seriousness. Having a family you adore is never a joke. It's the ultimate flex.

"Hey, real quick." West glances at me. "I heard you're a huge fan of The Burnt Clovers."

My mouth pops open as my gaze darts to Talon.

He holds up his hands and shrugs, but his eyes are filled with amusement.

"I—I am," I stutter.

West grins. "Good, because we got tickets to their Spring Break concert in Cancun and y'all are coming." He wags a finger between Talon and me. "See you guys later. Good game." West smacks Talon's back.

I gape after him.

"Close your mouth, babe," Lincoln mutters.

My jaw snaps shut, and I turn wide eyes to Talon.

"Seriously?" I ask.

"Seriously," he says, wrapping an arm around me and pulling me back against his chest. He dips his head to press a kiss to my temple.

"You're gonna discover your Irish roots," I murmur.

At that, Talon barks out a laugh, drawing curious glances from his teammates.

But Lincoln just grins. "It's the real deal," she says.

"Forever," Talon agrees, catching her drift.

I beam up at him in response and he kisses me hard.

"Oh, God, get a room, you two," Cohen jokes.

"Like you're one to talk," Avery grumbles.

Lincoln snorts in response.

But Talon and I ignore them all as I deepen our kiss.

I'm savoring this feeling of being wrapped up in our little bubble. In being loved on by Talon Miller.

EPILOGUE
TALON

Two Years Later

"What is it?" Leni asks, biting her bottom lip. She shakes the box and frowns, unable to guess the sound that's banging around inside.

"Open it." I nudge the gift closer. I can't wait to see her reaction.

She smirks at me before ripping into the paper like a little kid. "You know my birthday isn't for another few months."

"I know," I say. "This isn't a birthday gift. It's a just because gift."

"Just because what?" she wonders.

"Just because I love you," I say simply. "And March is our best window. I don't have football and wedding season is slow." Since Leni launched her wedding planning business just over a year ago, she's been unbelievably busy.

Between her New York City experience, her network through the debutante ball's organizing committee, and her internet fame for publicly calling out Craig, brides have flocked to work with her for their rustic chic, Tennessee weddings.

"So, we're going somewhere?" Leni presses.

I laugh. "Just open the box."

She sighs and lifts the lid. I love the frown that pinches her lips. "They're…snow boots." She holds up one of the white boots with gray fur and pompoms.

"They are," I agree.

"Are we going skiing?" She purses her lips.

I shrug. "I don't know. Are we?"

"Talon!" Leni snorts, swatting me adorably.

I lean closer and brush a kiss over her lips. "Think, Sunny Leni. Where would you wear snow boots?"

Concentration washes over her expression and then, a burst of excitement shines through. "Talon," I hear the hope in her tone and relief floods through me.

"Open the envelope," I suggest.

She tears into it and when she reads the airline tickets, she squeals. "Oh my God!" Leni launches herself into my arms.

I catch her, hugging her to my chest.

"We're going to the Arctic Circle! We're going to see the Northern Lights!" She waves the tickets in her hand wildly.

"We leave in a week." Her enthusiasm is contagious.

"I can't believe this," she murmurs. "This is my dream."

"I know." I run a hand over her hair.

She turns to face me, her expression bathed in love and light. Pure sunshine. "Thank you, Talon. I love you."

"I love you too, Leni," I say, kissing her.

She shifts her weight forward until I rock back, and she pins me beneath her. Straddling me, Leni grins. "I am seriously in shock right now. I can't believe we're doing my dream. Together."

"Believe it, Sunny." I grin up at her.

When she lowers her head again, our kiss morphs from sweet to needy. I'll never get enough of her. We make love on our living room floor, in the middle of a Tuesday, and I don't bother telling her that we're already doing my dream together. That meeting her, falling for her, has changed my outlook on life and reorganized priorities.

In fact, we've already crossed off the top item on my bucket list.

And I love working through every item on hers. Together. Forever.

I hope you loved Leni and Talon's romance! Have you been waiting ages for Avery Callaway's story? It's finally his turn! I've been wanting to redeem the infamous quarterback who broke Mila's heart in Hot Shot's Mistake for a long time. Avery's story is up next and I am thrilled to share that Bound and Blitzed releases in January! You can preorder it here.

ALSO BY GINA AZZI

Knoxville Coyotes Football:

Faked and Fumbled

Surprised and Sacked

Trapped and Tackled

The Burnt Clovers Trilogy:

Rebellious Rockstar

Resentful Rockstar

Restless Rockstar

Tennessee Thunderbolts:

Hot Shot's Mistake

Brawler's Weakness

Rookie's Regret

Playboy's Reward

Hero's Risk

Bad Boy's Downfall

Lock 'em Down

Boston Hawks Hockey:

The Sweet Talker

The Risk Taker

The Faker

The Rule Maker

The Defender

The Heart Chaser

The Trailblazer

The Hustler

The Score Keeper

Second Chance Chicago Series:

Broken Lies

Twisted Truths

Saving My Soul

Healing My Heart

The Kane Brothers Series:

Rescuing Broken (Jax's Story)

Recovering Beauty (Carter's Story)

Reclaiming Brave (Denver's Story)

My Christmas Wish

(A Kane Family Christmas

+ *One Last Chance* FREE prequel)

Finding Love in Scotland Series:

My Christmas Wish

(A Kane Family Christmas

+ *One Last Chance* FREE prequel)

One Last Chance (Daisy and Finn)

This Time Around (Aaron and Everly)

One Great Love

The College Pact Series:

The Last First Game (Lila's Story)

Kiss Me Goodnight in Rome (Mia's Story)

All the While (Maura's Story)

Me + You (Emma's Story)

Standalone

Corner of Ocean and Bay

ABOUT THE AUTHOR

Gina Azzi writes Contemporary and Sports Romance with relatable, genuine characters experiencing real life, love, friendships, and challenges. Dive into her sports romance series: Knoxville Coyotes Football, Boston Hawks Hockey, and Tennessee Thunderbolts, or get lost in her rockstar romances in The Burnt Clovers trilogy.

A Jersey girl at heart, Gina has spent her twenties traveling the world, living and working abroad, before settling down in Ontario, Canada with her husband and three children. She's a voracious reader, daydreamer, and coffee enthusiast who loves meeting new people.

Connect with her on social media or through www.ginaazzi.com.